SHADOWS ON THE THIRD FLOOR

BY

SANDRA S. ROSE

TABLE OF CONTENTS

CHAPTER 1: 1800 MILES TO HOME..................................... 1

CHAPTER 2: FAMILY PORTRAIT 4

CHAPTER 3: HOME WAS NEVER LIKE THIS........................ 8

CHAPTER 4: THE INHERITANCE.................................... 10

CHAPTER 5: INTRODUCTION TO STUART MANOR....... 16

CHAPTER 6: PERMISSION GRANTED 22

CHAPTER 7: WHAT WAS THAT?..................................... 24

CHAPTER 8: SINISTER SURPRISE................................... 28

CHAPTER 9: THE PINK DRESS....................................... 32

CHAPTER 10: THE PLAN 36

CHAPTER 11: THE SECRET SEARCH 38

CHAPTER 12: INTRUDER ALERT 42

CHAPTER 13: RESUMING THE SEARCH.......................... 48

CHAPTER 14: CHANGING THE RULES............................ 51

CHAPTER 15: ELUSIVE KEYS 55

CHAPTER 16: RHYME OR REASON................................ 58

CHAPTER 17: SHADOWS AND MUSIC............................ 64

CHAPTER 18: BEYOND THE VEIL.................................. 69

CHAPTER 19: PART-TIME SLEUTHS............................... 75

CHAPTER 20: FINDING CELESTE 79

CHAPTER 21: THE LOCKET 85

CHAPTER 22: THE EXODUS.. 90

ABOUT THE AUTHOR 96

BOOKS BY THIS AUTHOR.. 97

CHAPTER 1:

1800 MILES TO HOME

With the steam whistle blaring a warning to all who remain on the Houston station platform and passengers not yet seated, the gigantic iron locomotive rumbles to life. It thunders forward, shaking the ground beneath and belching great clouds of steam as it begins the journey. With herculean power, the mighty engine tugs each car into its place in the caravan behind and begins to gather speed.

DESTINATION: Boston, an inheritance, century-old traditions, and eerie examples of BIZARRE - waiting in the SHADOWS ON THE THIRD FLOOR.

Inside one of the first-class passenger cars, the Conductor begins his duties. He balances like an expert while walking down the long aisle of the swaying car, checking all boarding tickets. He boastfully estimates the trains' speed will soon reach more than 60 miles an hour as twelve-year-old Lizzy Stuart stops him to ask questions. Quickly calculating, Lizzie is pleased that the family's trip may be quicker than she thought. "Imagine, 60 miles an hour! she thinks, "if Boston is Eighteen Hundred miles away, we can be there in just a few days."

Today marks the Stuart family's first trip by railroad. Mrs. Stuarts' intense fear of flying made travel by train their only option. Hence, everything about this experience is a new adventure for these novice travelers.

Marshal and Jessica Stuart try to be a little lenient about the children's understandable excitement while still insisting that these three "busybodies" remember their manners, including proper respect for other passengers. A task as much doomed to failure as "herding cats."

Intently, the children watch as passengers surrender their tickets to the Conductor, into which he carefully punches a small hole and hands it back. He looks like he must be a very important man. He wears a smart-looking black uniform with a gold braid on his cap and on the sleeves of his jacket, which also sports bright gold buttons. He looks very much like a policeman from back home in Texas. Yes, he must be crucial indeed.

Lizzy, her 9-year-old Brother Kevin and their 5-year-old Sister Darlene are so excited they can barely sit still. Boston will be their new home, though the question remains as to why their parents have chosen to make a move so suddenly. With very little notice, the children are pulled from school, and preparations made to have their lessons for the remainder of the school year forwarded to the new address. Their Mother intends to see that the lessons continue at home, with testing completed at the local school.

Boston is where their Fathers' Mother lives, and they have not seen Grandmother Hannah in over a year. The children remember her as a kind but pragmatic woman. However, she is sweet, and they are overjoyed at the prospect of seeing her again. Her annual flights to visit were so enjoyable because she always stayed for at least two weeks that just never seemed to be long enough. A-Pillar of the community and member of the Boston Elite, Hannah Stuart relocated to Stuart Manor as a temporary agent following the premature death of her husband a year ago. She manages the estates' affairs until the new heir can be verified and contractually installed into the position.

Lizzy and Kevin occupy much of their time trying to unravel the mystery surrounding the sudden trip to Boston, with no information from their parents during the next few days. Perhaps their father has been offered a partnership with a more prominent law firm in Boston, or maybe he feels neglectful of his now-widowed Mother. Whatever the reason, they will be happy to see Grandmother Hannah again.

"Remember the sugar donuts she baked for us during her last visit?" Lizzy said, licking her lips and rolling her eyes at the thought of having those fresh, warm delights once again.

"Oh boy, do I" exclaimed Kevin. "I hope she has not forgotten how to make them. Gosh, just thinking about them makes our mouths water. Mother tried to make them, but obviously, Grandmothers are just better cooks."

"I hope she lets us explore her attic as we did at home," Lizzy said as she imagined their grandmother living in an old creaky, wooden house with an attic full of boxes and old relics. "It was fun pretending that the old things we found were real treasures. Grandmothers' attic must be running over with things a lot older than what we had. Maybe we can even find a dark secret or one of those skeletons father said some people have in a closet. I never really understood why people would keep secrets and skeletons in a closet, but he said they do, so it must be true."

The children continue to reminisce about Grandmother Hannah's visits. Pleasant memories pass time and halt, at least for a little while, their concern over the urgency of their trip. Lizzy, being the eldest, is understandably a little more worried about her parents and hoping to find some way to help. On the other hand, her father is both worried and excited, leaving Lizzy confused. After all, if something is an emergency, wouldn't he be either very sad or thrilled? During Grandmother's call, he and Mother received startling news, but everything has been so hectic since there has been no time for explanations. What could have happened so suddenly to induce their father to leave his law practice with Faulkner and Stuart and move his family clear across the country? Whatever the reason is, timing must be an essential part of the answer because of the hurried way her parents arranged the move.

CHAPTER 2:

FAMILY PORTRAIT

Marshal Stuart; Born 1917 in Boston, Husband, Father, successful lawyer. An attractive man but not quite matinée idol material.

Lovable, reasonably strict, but not harsh. A traditional, stubborn, and sometimes intolerant conservative, he is well-liked and respected by his peers. High intelligence and equally high work and moral ethic have earned him much success in his professional and private life.

Marshal graduated from Harvard Law School in 1942, tried to enlist in the Navy when Pearl Harbor was attacked but failed because he had a wife and child. He began practicing law with a firm in Texas and remained there for the past twelve years. Now, with this sudden but necessary move back to his hometown of Boston, his exact plans take a hard turn into the unexpected.

Jessica Stuart, wife and mother of three children, was born in 1920 in Boston and married Marshal Stuart shortly after graduation. Jessica is a tall, beautiful woman with a classic Slender profile, soft voice, and calming influence on those around her. Her large brown eyes add to her youthful appearance, an attribute her eldest daughter has inherited. She is wearing her Soft shoulder-length light brown hair in a modest daytime bun style, and her facial features have little need for cosmetics.

Full of sweet Christian charity, she follows her own advice - "if you can't say something nice about someone, don't say anything at all." A tolerant, loving mother and homemaker whose life is about to change in ways she never imagined.

Elizabeth (Lizzy) Stuart: like most Twelve-year-old girls, she is curious about almost everything. Her father's sudden decision to move the family to Boston is as exciting as it is mysterious. She cannot pretend that she likes feeling uprooted away from her friends and

4

summer plans. But obviously, this situation is more critical for the family, so there's no time for pouting.

Lizzy is a bold young lady. Outgoing, energetic, intelligent, and honest to a fault. She makes friends quickly, so it seems she never meets a stranger. She is also too strong-willed for her own good, which gets her in trouble from time to time. Unfortunately, she has a very vivid imagination and is inclined to daydream, which frustrates her teachers and is why her grades are seldom better than a B in any subject other than Art. Seemingly, her daydreams are fed ideas and feasible "whodunits" by her steady diet of Nancy Drew mystery stories. Lizzy hopes to be a writer one day, but her parents insist she finish her education first.

Not an unattractive girl, but it appears it may be a few years before her femininity surfaces enough to change her interests and appearance. Tomboyish! Yes, tomboyish is an excellent way to begin describing Lizzy's apparent "in-between" phase. Her Five feet Five-inch lanky, slender frame suggests she will likely surpass her mother's statuesque form. Her huge brown eyes cannot escape notice as they exaggerate her every facial expression. Her long, light brown hair is worn pulled back, and tied with a wide powder blue ribbon that matches her freshly pressed dress. With white gloves, stockings, and Patent leather Mary Jane style shoes, the look successfully disguises the rambunctious, pigtail wearing, tree climbing youth under the flower trimmed hat.

One day soon, her curiosity will be tested, and she will long for the comfort and security of her daydreams.

Kevin Stuart: Born 1945, and like his big sister, he is very curious by nature but is more intellectual than she, much to the delight of his parents. Five feet Zero inches, and wiry with dark brown hair worn to model after his father's short, collegiate style. His eyes are brown, like his parents, but not as big and expressive as Lizzy's, for which he is thankful. His slender form is still very much child-like in appearance with protruding shoulder blades, narrow chest, and seems to be all arms and legs. He resembles his father in the face and promises to be quite attractive once he grows into his bony frame. Farsighted, he wears

5

glasses for his school work and hobbies, though he really dislikes them and often misplaces them on purpose.

Kevin has a keen intellect for his age which accounts for his honor roll grades. He is energetic and enjoys exploring very much when he has the opportunity. Kevin likes playing chess with his father at home and sometimes even beats Lizzy at a game. Reading and bicycling with his friends are his favorite hobbies but building model airplanes is a real passion, probably because he hopes to be a flier himself one day. Though usually quiet and easy to get along with, Kevin sometimes exhibits his father's stubborn, intolerant attitude, but also, like his father, it never lasts very long. Understandably, he is not pleased with having to leave his buddies and school back in Texas. However, he has agreed to make the new changes with as little fuss as possible.

He will wish he and Lizzy hadn't gone exploring...to the Third Floor soon.

Darlene Stuart: a little small for Five years old with delicate features and inclined to be a "girly-girl." Curly light brown hair, brown eyes, and eyelashes most girls will be jealous of someday. She looks forward to kindergarten in Boston.

A curious and busy little girl, she loves picture books and learning her ABCs. She spends a few hours every afternoon after nap time, sitting on the sofa, pretending to teach "Pony," her tattered, gray stuffed toy pony, how to read. Darlene, or "Dee," as her family calls her, entertains herself most of the time except when her father sits down to read the evening newspaper. Now it's Dee's time with Dad. Making herself comfortable in his lap with "Pony" in one arm, she enjoys a quiet half-hour break from play. In her innocence, Darlene doesn't quite understand the changes, but she doesn't mind as long as everyone and everything she loves is nearby.

Grandmother Hannah Stuart: Born in 1894, Marshal's Mother and Grandmother of the Stuart children. A handsome woman for her age, with a slightly overweight but striking figure, dark brown hair sporting a gray streak that accents a wave in her stylish hairdo close to her face, and soft brown eyes which reflect her love for her family. A strong,

Intelligent, and assertive Christian woman who enjoys a good-spirited argument once in a while.

Hannah was born at the turn of the century when women, still subjugated, depended upon their husbands for their living and were not permitted to vote or seek employment until August of 1920. She could have chosen a life to match her ambition if not for the culture of her time. Hannah Stuart knows that Stuart Manor will need the family to make many lifestyle changes, but she has no idea how many changes remain behind locked doors and waiting on the Third Floor.

CHAPTER 3:

HOME WAS NEVER LIKE THIS

Finally, following three and a half days of travel, the colossal locomotive lumbers to a stop at the Boston station platform. Giving what resembles a giant sigh of relief, it again belches immense clouds of steam while conductors and porters rush to retrieve luggage and packages for the disembarking passengers.

Waiting on the platform for Marshal and the family is Grandmother Hannah and her driver. At last, the children bound out of the train, running and squealing to give Grandmother the hugs and kisses they have been saving up for over a year. As eager as the children, Jessica and Marshal share the joy of seeing Mother again and confess relief at the end of their journey. Little do they know; *this is just the beginning.*

Now that the luggage is claimed and loaded into the trunk of the black limousine, they are on their way for the comfortable thirty-minute trip home. With the car windows down at the children's request, the warm Spring air is a much appreciated change from the atmosphere in the confining railroad cars.

Lizzy is listening carefully to the adult conversations while they ride, hopefully grasping some insight into the mystery surrounding the long trip from Texas, which seemed to take weeks instead of days. But she can only hear partial sentences, not enough to understand. The curious twelve-year-old plans to ask her parents for more details when they have some time alone. However, she has to pick her time very carefully because even in 1954, children are not privy to information or decisions discussed by adults. They are just barely beyond the recently foregone "children are meant to be seen and not heard" rules of social conduct for young people.

Soon, the limousine turns onto a wide pebble driveway and through a large black iron gate. All that can be heard now are the small stones beneath the weight of the grand limousine, with no one saying a word. Grandmother Hannah says nothing, watching and listening for the family's reactions. There was no way to prepare them, so explanations will come when the initial shock wears off.

Everything becomes still inside the car as the occupants stare at the surrounding grounds and gardens on the way to the main house. Beautifully manicured lawns, shrubbery, and flowers as far as the eye can see. And looking past the driver and through the front windshield, they see Stuart Manor looming in the distance. A vast, three-story Country Manor Home, built in 1803 by Marshals' Great, Great Grandfather, Sir Reginald Stuart.

Sir Reginald built the home shortly after his appointment to Diplomatic service by President Andrew Jackson. The newly re-established relations with Britain presented an opportunity for Sir Reginald to admire the Seventeenth and Eighteenth-century homes of the titled Elite. He vowed to build one similar in Boston upon his return.

The closer they drive to the white Manor, the more beautiful, imposing, and formidable it appears. Arriving at the front doors, Lizzy stretches through the open window of the limousine to look upward as the enormous structure seems to grow, with its three stories reaching skyward and large, single-story wings attached to the North and south ends of the great Manor. The portico they stop under is supported by four massive white columns that resemble the Plantations of the Seventeenth and eighteenth centuries in the South.

Once the family exits the limousine, three men appear to carry the luggage to the second-floor bedrooms. Before entering, the new residents turn to look once more and marvel at the landscape before them, nearly speechless in their surprise. Even the children are reasonably quiet - a rare but welcome silence. So many questions need answers, and Hannah promises to address all of their concerns tomorrow. For tonight, everyone will wash off the dust of travel and then relax and enjoy a splendid meal before bedtime.

CHAPTER 4:

THE INHERITANCE

Rising at Seven O'clock and hearing his mother's voice coming from downstairs as she issues instructions to the staff, Marshal finds he is only the second one awake and ready for breakfast. He wants to let his wife and children sleep as long as they need to. Everyone was so exhausted from the trip; he was surprised that he didn't sleep a while longer. But even the trip and delicious dinner couldn't induce sound sleep when his thoughts were still crowding his mind with unanswered questions about the urgent need for him at Stuart Manor. He and his wife were already considering moving back to their home State, but Hannah's call had pushed the couple's plans up on their priority calendar.

Marshal descends the long staircase, admiring the rubbed mahogany rails and looking forward to an excellent leisurely breakfast with his mother. A little lost in the massive hallway at the bottom of the stairs, he follows her voice and enters the familiar small dining room where the family dined casually the night before. Greeting his mother with a kiss on the forehead, he obeys her gesture to help himself to the food on the sideboard along the wall. Such a large variety of breakfast delights, it seems only polite to try a little bit of everything, which he does, happily.

Hannah and her son engage in general small talk, news items, and local politics for the better part of an hour before Jessica and the children join them. Lizzy and Kevin eagerly help themselves to pancakes and fruit before choosing seats close to Grandmother while Jessica prepares helpings for Dee and herself.

After breakfast, the well-rested, alert, and fed children are looking for something to do, so Marshal sends the three of them outside to explore the grounds closest to the building. The adults go to the extensive library in the front of the manor, where they can watch the children through the massive windows along the front wall.

Hannah is about to clarify the mystery surrounding Stuart Manor and the family when Peggy, one of the three downstairs maids, enters and exits the large room quietly, leaving behind fresh coffee and the morning mail on the table near the window as instructed earlier.

Hannah begins by explaining to Marshal how the history of Stuart Manor, the endowments, properties, and the Stuart family's progression as owners and caretakers are intertwined.

"Well, I suppose it is best to give you as much information about the origin of this home as I can. Considering this information chronologically, may make it easier to understand. We can fit all the puzzle pieces together once you have a general idea of the overall picture. After lunch, we can tour the home and grounds." Hannah produces a typewritten paper from the desk; "Here you are, Marshal. You can follow along with me, and then you will have this list to refer to later."

Marshal listens intently as his mother explains the historical procession of Stuart Manor's heirs. He is thankful to have something tangible to reference while the lawyer side of his brain tries to sort out the information related to his mother and family. He often learned bits and pieces of information about the family and the lavish home, but Uncle Howard, his father's elder brother, had been the legal heir since 1933.

Great, Great, Great Grandfather Reginald Stuart had the manor built in 1803 and cared for it until 1890. Then his son, Marshal's Great Grandfather, inherited all of the properties, the endowments, farms, and livestock until he died in 1912. Afterward, Marshal's Grandfather inherited everything until he died in 1933, and then everything went to Uncle Howard. Last February, Uncle Howard unexpectedly passed away and had no male children, so his brother, Marshal's Father, inherited the properties. Unfortunately, a few months later, Marshal Stuart Senior also passed away. So, Marshal's Mother, the estate lawyer, and the bank's consultant have been taking care of the estates' business

11

until the new heir can, at last, be confirmed with contracts signed and filed.

"Of course, you understand now that you are the legal heir of the estate, and so there is much for you to do and learn," Hannah says with grave seriousness. "I won't try to minimize the importance of what fate has handed you, and I know this is not what you foresaw for your future, but you must carry on in your father's place and keep the Stuart Manor thriving. The surrounding village and business community depend on its survival. One day Kevin will be old enough and wise enough to step into your shoes. While growing up here, he will learn all he needs to know about the estate and its responsibilities."

Marshal turns to watch his son chasing the girls on the front lawn and making monster faces that delight little Dee, giggling as she runs as fast as her chubby little legs will carry her. A new game, invented by the three of them to enjoy the outdoors and still obey their father's instructions to stay close to the manor. Slightly overwhelmed, he realizes that the boy will have less than twelve years to enjoy his childhood and schooling before taking up the mantle of partial responsibility for Stuart Manor while grooming for the eventuality of full responsibility as heir. For a moment Marshal is both sad for his son and proud of what he will become. Kevin's future and Stuart Manor will be secure when Marshal signs the contracts, already scheduled for next week.

"There's something else you need to know, which is one reason we must act quickly," Hannah says, interrupting her sons' concentration. "You see, a generous portion of the household income is provided through cooperation with Massachusetts' State Tourism Office. Beginning in late Spring through fall of each year, Stuart Manor is open to tourist groups by appointment only. They usually arrive by motorcoach with Forty-Five passengers each, and we average four to five groups a month. One full day, three times a year, we are open to local visitors. We coordinate with the village businesses so that half a dozen set up their booths along the side of the driveway, three at each end of the building. Six businesses in the Spring, Summer, and fall."

"Good Golly Mother, when did the tourism start," Marshal blurted out, laughing at his own surprise.

"Two years ago, when your Uncle Howard contacted your father and me for suggestions to bring in a little more money for household expenses," Hannah replied. "I'm afraid it was my idea," she said modestly. "I used to drive over and help get things organized until we had enough staff and volunteers to handle the crowds. But it does help with expenses, and Lord knows, there's enough of that with this huge property."

"Oh, I think it is a fine idea, Mother," Marshal assures her. "I am just a little surprised. I would never have thought of it." Marshal smiles at his mother's ingenuity with approval while he remembers growing up with this woman who could and would, do just about anything she put her mind to.

Jessica, listening to the conversation while keeping an eye on the children, now motions for them to come back inside for a while. Lizzy gathers up her two siblings and herds them into the library to their mother's side.

"I'm delighted you weren't wearing your good clothes out there," Jessica says with a teasing smile as she picks pieces of grass and dirt from Dee's dress. With a tone of understanding in her voice, she sends the children to the second floor to wash up and change. Without hesitation, her brood sprints toward the staircase and disappears on the floor above.

Jessica rises and begins strolling toward the far end of the large room, contemplating everything her Mother-In-Law has just explained. She examines the rooms' contents and is impressed by the endless display of fine literature and invaluable binders of information on bookcase shelves. Embroidered wall hangings and exquisite paintings hang high on each wall and, therefore, are appreciated from all room angles.

Marshal has not yet asked for her opinion, but Jessica knows her husband is hoping for some sign of approval for this drastic change in the couples' plans for their family. She also knows that what they have

13

discussed so far is just the tip of the iceberg. Jessica is acutely aware that to introduce objections at this point could be an irreparable blow to her marriage, the Stuart family, and the community. Therefore, to Hannah's surprise, she announces that whatever path her husband chooses, she and her children will be at his side, and she offers to do what she can to help Stuart Manor and the Community.

"Oh, my dear," exclaims Hannah, "That's wonderful news, and I appreciate your support so much."

Marshal takes his wife's hands in his, and with a look in his eyes only she recognizes, he expresses his appreciation, knowing full well that his wife has just set her plans and desires to one side for the good of something more crucial to others.

"Well then," says Hannah, "I had better speak to Mrs. Kelly about having all of the staff in the Servants Hall for the meeting following lunch. They must become acquainted with their new employers' family. It is also critical that you familiarize yourself with the people who will be present in your daily lives from now on. Eventually, everyone will adjust and develop trust and a proper working relationship. Okay, I will see you all back downstairs at lunch in about Thirty minutes."

"See you in a little while, Mother," says Marshal as Hannah rushes off to remind the Housekeeper about the planned staff meeting. "Jessica and I are going upstairs to talk to the children. We promised to answer some of their questions, and we know they are going to be excited, so we will try to keep the noise down."

The children react almost precisely as predicted, but a few decibels less than expected. Lizzy seems genuinely stunned at the news of her father's inheritance and his new position. Soon after their arrival, Lizzy assumed that her little family of Five would probably be living in another house, possibly somewhere on the grounds, but surely not in this enormous manor. Now it seems, she and Kevin will need to learn how to navigate the many rooms, doors, and hallways without getting lost. But Marshal reassures them that they will attend the staff meeting and tour the house with himself and their mother. Together,

Grandmother Hannah and Mrs. Kelly will conduct them through the endless labyrinth of passageways and chambers of the three floors and underground rooms of their magnificent new home.

"Alright, family," Marshal says cheerfully. "Let's go down to lunch and then see what other surprises await us this afternoon." Very happy with the way their children are cooperating and adjusting, Jessica and Marshal herd their little group down to the dining room.

CHAPTER 5:

INTRODUCTION TO STUART MANOR

Following lunch, the family joins Mrs. Kelly and the other employees in the servant's hall downstairs. The staff of Nineteen, all employed by the Stuart family for at least eight years, seem content in their positions. Marshal attempts to draw each one out during brief introductions and discovers that Twelve of the nineteen have family ties to staff members of the original Nineteenth-century Stuart Manor and referred the remaining Seven for employment. Marshal and Jessica are impressed by this prevalent theme, which seems to bond the workers together in cooperation with the Stuart family. What could be better than to have their first staff meeting conclude on such a positive note! Everyone returns to work with the promise of an active open-door policy for all who request appointments through Mrs. Kelly.

Tour of the home begins underground with brief visits to the kitchen areas of meal preparation and huge food storage pantry. Refrigerated lockers are next, with the laundry, sewing room, boot room (for cleaning and care of shoes and leather riding equipment), offices of the Housekeeper and Maintenance Supervisors, linen and uniform storage, table settings room containing silver and China, wine cellar, boiler room and ample room for storage of surplus household furniture, etc. Five servants' quarters and facilities remain empty, clean, and available for use now that all but the Housekeeper, Butler, Cook, and Kitchen Assistant live in the village.

Lizzy and Kevin take notice of the layout of the underground rooms and how inviting some of them are for great explorers such as themselves. With three more stories and an attic yet to consider, it seems this enormous residence will provide many opportunities for their favorite pastime. Both children become more and more attentive

16

to the tour, anxious to locate and memorize the location of all nooks and crannies. They agree to meet in the small library at the end of the day to map out every area of interest they intend to investigate.

The main level of Manor homes is nearly always a traditional exercise in extravagance, and Stuart Manor is no exception. This area reflects the head of the household status through the plush furnishings and desirable collections of fine art, including prized sculptures and other cultural groups indicative of the Seventeenth, Eighteenth, and Nineteenth Centuries. The structured interior proudly displays many hand-carved accents in the opulent ceilings, walls, doors, pillars, gallery, and staircases just as they did centuries earlier.

The family deliberately slows the pace of the tour to absorb as much of each room's character as possible with a brief, get acquainted stroll through the complex network of rooms and corridors. It will take some time before everyone can travel from point A to point B without the embarrassment of getting lost in route.

"Mother, do you happen to know where the blueprints for this house might be?" asks Marshal, with extreme doubt that any such blueprints would still exist on a house built in 1803.

"No, but we have something just as helpful," Hannah says, giggling at her son's apparent exasperation. "There are pamphlets with detailed maps of the interior ready to display in the foyer for this next Tourist Season. I suggest each of you carry one in your pocket until you know your way around."

"That's a relief Mother Stuart," says Jessica. "I've been a little worried that Lizzy or Kevin may get lost and panic. They both love to explore, and it would be just like them to get in a predicament and can't find their way out. Dee isn't a concern because she stays near me all day."

Marshal, satisfied that there is a reliable map available, is content to continue the tour while resolving to make daily trips through the home on his own until entirely familiar with the location and contents of each room on every floor. He advises Jessica, Lizzy, and Kevin to do the same to save embarrassment later.

17

The family continues to canvass all areas carefully, including the extensive library with reading area combined with Marshal's office facilities, a small library with reading area, formal dining room, informal dining and breakfast room, formal living room, sitting room, art, and artifacts, reception area, ballroom, billiards and game room and finally, the gun room. Also, everyone was made aware of the corridors and stairwells used by the servants to have access to each floor without disturbing residents and guests.

Having completed the tour of the main floor rooms, the family inspects the attached wings at the North and south ends of the manor. Each attachment is a charming two-bedroom, fully furnished cottage. The North cottage has access to the main house through the billiards room, while the South cottage has access through the reading area of the extensive library. Seldom used, they are available to overnight guests who may have difficulty navigating the fatiguing staircase to the second floor in the manor house or nursing a guest who becomes ill during their visit.

After visiting every area of the two levels, taking a much-needed break and a few minutes for coffee and conversation, the group ascends to the second-floor gallery to inspect the eight huge bedrooms and nursery. As every bedroom is identical except for furnishings, motif, and such, the tour is complete. When examining the nursery, Hannah approaches Marshal and Jessica with a suggestion for their approval.

"I have been thinking that with the tourism season due to begin, and the work demanded of all of us to make it a success, would you consider hiring a Nanny to supervise the children? Not an older woman like we would normally need for babies in the house, but a younger, experienced girl who could help with their studies and supervise their recreation, including hosting social interactions with their schoolmates. Lizzy is of an age to enjoy pajama parties and lunches with her girlfriends from school. And most importantly, Nanny would watch over the welfare of the children while all the adults are busy. Jessica, you are used to devoting the majority of your time to your children, and the reality is, time with them will be limited, and you will need the help. We can't just send the children off to play when we're busy, especially Dee. They won't understand and crave adult attention, even though the two older ones will understand the situation. We can advertise, but we won't hire until you approve a candidate. What do you think?"

Though she had thought of this after committing herself to help with the tourism project, Jessica is surprised that the question arises at this time and stammers through her reply. "Mother Stuart, I have considered the possibility before this, but Marshal and I need time to discuss the idea before moving forward. Please give us a few days to think it over."

"Of course, my dear, and I promise, you will have the last word on the subject," Hannah says in a sincere and reassuring tone, trying not to infringe on the couple's parental authority.

"Well, what do you say we go up to the third floor? There really isn't that much up there, and I don't see any need to go into the attic. Therefore, we can take a quick look upstairs and have time to wash up before dinner," Hannah suggests as she sends Mrs. Kelly back down to the kitchens to make sure that dinner will be ready to serve in about an hour.

With the welcome news that the family tour is nearly ending, they climb the stairs to the floor above with new enthusiasm. The staff has anticipated that dusk would begin at about this stage of the tour and has already turned the lights on in the third-floor gallery. Hannah begins their inspection at the far end of the hallway so that she can turn the lights off as they head back toward the staircase.

The third floor has a grim, empty, and almost foreboding atmosphere due to nonuse, limited lighting, and the obnoxious presence of a thick layer of dust everywhere.

Rooms line the hallway from one end to the other, with doors tightly closed and locked and no outside light. One room at the end is unlocked and filled with various old luggage, many cardboard boxes of different sizes, and several large, heavy trunks. Hannah explains, "I think it is a shame that the previous heirs just let this part of the house go unused. The story goes that these rooms were frequently used when

Stuart Manor hosted visiting politicians and other dignitaries until about mid-1807 when tragedy turned Stuart's life upside down. A fire swept through almost the entire floor one night while the family hosted a large dinner and dance for charity. Sixty of the guests and Stuarts' eight-year-old daughter, Celeste, perished that night. When the area was reconstructed, evidence was found that proved the fire was deliberately set, but the culprit was never apprehended. The theory remains to this day that Miss Celeste wandered into the third-floor hallway and saw a footman named Tucker carry a can of kerosene and a lit candle to the other end of the hall and start the fire. He panicked and locked her inside before running down the stairs to safety. During reconstruction, the room key was found at the bottom of the stairs and a footman's white-glove only a few feet away. The strangest thing is, Tucker was never found, but there have been several reports of hearing him walk from room to room but never leaving the third floor. Rumor insists that Tucker had second thoughts and ran back into the fire to rescue Celeste but perished with the others. The locals believe that his ghost and the other poor souls who died that night are condemned to roam within those rooms forever unless released by a family relative with the original key.

Shortly after the construction ended, the family locked everything up and refused to open the area up again. Then, the excuse was that the new key to the rooms had been lost, and with the household below having everything it needed, gaining entry was never necessary. The locked rooms may be empty, though I have no way of knowing at present, so calling a locksmith to make a key just hasn't been a priority."

With a quick glance at one another, Lizzy and Kevin know they have just found the perfect place and reason to begin their exploration, and they can hardly wait to get started. Lizzy lets the information soak into her brain, unable to understand how anyone would allow the entire third floor of this beautiful home go to waste. It could be a splendid addition to the rest of the house once it is cleaned properly. Who locked the rooms? A century and a half? Really? One Hundred and Fifty years? Have these doors been locked for at least One Hundred years? Locking it all up while they grieved the loss of their daughter is perfectly understandable, but leaving it unattended for so long is such a waste. As far as the rumors about Tucker's ghost goes, well, that's just absurd. There's no such thing as ghosts. She and Kevin must find that key and ghosts or no ghosts; they've got to get inside these locked rooms! Who knows, maybe there's a million dollars or a bag of valuable jewels hidden somewhere or maybe clues to a hidden treasure on the estate grounds!

"Holy smoke," exclaims Lizzy, holding her voice to a whisper. Her face flushes pink with excitement at the realization of the possibilities. "They have to be kidding; I mean, it's ridiculous. Who's going to leave rooms just locked up for over a century? It makes no sense at all." Suddenly, the color drains from Lizzy's face, and her expression changes at the realization that maybe the answer they need ISN'T WHO, BUT WHY! Why would anyone lock those doors and leave them year after year? What don't they want anyone to see? "The key isn't lost…it is hidden," Lizzy blurts out loud. She and Kevin need to find it or convince Grandmother Hannah or their father to hire a locksmith.

"Lizzy, this is incredible! We have to start first thing in the morning with the open room," whispers Kevin, and the two shake hands in excited agreement. With imaginations running wild, the two explorers will barely sleep tonight.

With the other four anxious to leave the gloomy, ominous atmosphere of the third floor, Lizzy and Kevin would rather remain to begin their adventure tonight by going through the luggage, trunks, and every inch of the musty, old, and neglected room. However, it is just about dinner time, and Grandmother Hannah would be upset if they ask to stay behind, and they will need her permission to return in the morning. Tonight, the two pint-sized detectives need to agree on a plan.

CHAPTER 6:

PERMISSION GRANTED

The following day, Lizzy and Kevin leave their rooms almost 7simultaneously and laugh at the coincidence as they reach the top of the stairs together and hurry down to breakfast. They are the first to arrive in the dining room, but the sideboard is laden with half a dozen food warmers, and everything smells so delicious.

Beside themselves with anticipation, the keyed-up pair of detectives fight the urge to gulp their food down. But they must wait for Grandmother Hannah and mind their manners, for they don't want to get on the wrong side of her, especially this morning. They need her permission to begin their search for clues concerning the history of the mysterious third floor.

Within a few minutes, Hannah and Marshal arrive and are a little surprised to see the children almost halfway through their breakfasts.

"Goodness me," their father exclaims. "I'm flabbergasted to see you two sleepy heads up and dressed already. You must have big plans for today."

"Yes, actually we do," replies Lizzy. "Kevin and I want to ask you and Grandmother Hannah for permission to go exploring on the third floor this morning. Maybe we can find out why all of those rooms are locked up. It's going to be so much fun."

"Well, I don't see why you shouldn't," says Marshall, delighted to see his children enthused again about their favorite pastime. "As long as it is alright with your grandmother, and you promise to be very careful up there."

"I don't mind at all," says Hannah. "However," she adds with a mischievous grin, "it seems to me that exploring is hard work, and you probably won't be finished by lunchtime, so go and ask Mrs. Kelly to

22

have a lunch packed to take with you. But mind you now, be sure to bathe and change clothes before coming back down to dinner this evening."

Relieved and happy, Lizzy and Kevin thank their grandmother and excuse themselves from the table to go in search of Mrs. Kelly. Dear Mrs. Kelly, always willing to help and never seems to mind the interruptions by a family new to the ways of the Manor. She is especially nice to provide milk and freshly baked cookies while the children wait for the carefully packed lunch and sodas they will take with them on their new adventure to the third floor.

While planning their first day, the young detectives decide to log anything they find that Grandmother Hannah may want to know about. Who knows, maybe they will find valuable antiques. But more importantly, they need to locate the key that unlocks the remaining rooms. Piles of gold coins, pearls, and other fine jewels fill the imagination and motivate the couple to begin their search in earnest.

With lunches and flashlights in hand, the children climb the stairs, turn the lights on in the gallery, and the open room at the end of the long unfamiliar hallway. Even with their flashlights, the area seems mysterious and threatening. However, their excitement and anticipation erase all fear, and they forge ahead, determined to rid the house of this enigma.

CHAPTER 7:

WHAT WAS THAT?

With expectations that they will make amazing discoveries before the day's end, they begin by clearing spaces to work. They move trunks, suitcases, cardboard boxes, and different odds and ends of old furniture to one side of the large dusty room. Then, by wiping off a couple of stools and using an empty trunk as a desk, they begin their search by rummaging through the contents of the first of many suitcases. Thoughts of possible discoveries feed their imaginations.

Three hours later, the pair are excited at the sight of a Military uniform, preserved for all these years with just a wrapping of tissue paper and the protection of the large, once sturdy suitcase with the two leather belts that fasten tightly around each end.

"Golly," exclaims both children as they lift a Nineteenth-Century Army Officer's Blue and red uniform jacket, white gloves, and white trousers from the case, followed by a spectacular large hat and black riding boots. A white sash with the empty scabbard lay at the bottom, completing the image of the brave officer. This find unexpectedly piques the children's curiosity with a wish to know more about the man who wore it into battle more than a hundred years ago. They re-check the case and quickly look around the room for signs of the missing sword but find no clue where it might be, providing it survived the battlefield.

Minor damage to the uniform encourages Lizzy to return the articles to the suitcase after some gentle brushing, hoping that Grandmother Hannah may wish to display it during the tourism season or donate it to the local museum. So, after returning everything carefully to the large case, securing it with the belts, and labeling the top with a list of the contents, Kevin carries it to a prepared room area. He logs the case as number one on the clipboard log he fashioned earlier. What a fabulous find to mark the first day of their adventure. "I hope we find some picture albums sometime soon," says Lizzy with a new found thirst for information about the unknown soldier and possibly Stuart family relatives of the same era.

Lizzy and Kevin continue to look through some of the smaller suitcases and boxes for another four hours after hungrily consuming the tasty lunch Mrs. Kelly had prepared for them. Everything was so delicious, and eating lunch away from the rest of the family made the whole day seem like hunting for prizes at a picnic or maybe a scavenger hunt. But the two hunters are getting tired and must go back to their rooms to wash up and change for dinner. So, they begin to clean around their work area and gather what they need to return downstairs.

"Shhhh, listen," Kevin demands suddenly. "What was that?"

"What was what?" Lizzy whispers with eyes wide open, holding her breath while she listens for the sound that alarms her brother.

"Shhh"! Kevin insists. "I heard something, and it came from that corner, over there, at the end of the room. Someone was walking across the floor. Where's that darned flashlight?" Kevin whispers as he nervously looks for the flashlight among the articles they brought upstairs with them. "The ceiling light bulb must have burned out over there. See? There's one that's not lit, and why that corner is so dark."

"I don't hear or see anything," Lizzy confesses quietly as she stares across the room into the darkness. Half of her is afraid to move, while her other half tries to convince her that her brothers' imagination has conjured up something that isn't there.

At last, Kevin locates the flashlight and shines the light into the dark corner, looking for anything that could have created the sound that took him by surprise. Perhaps it was an animal of some kind that's been living in the unused room, he thought. And convincing himself that this is the only logical reason for the sound reassures his sister with that simple explanation and suggests they call it a day and continue their quest after breakfast tomorrow. So, with the plan of beginning again bright and early the following day, they gather their paraphernalia and go to their rooms one flight below to wash up for dinner.

25

Once back in her bedroom, Lizzy realizes that the storeroom where she and Kevin have spent the day happens to be directly above. She remembers that her brother said he heard someone walking across the floor and then convinced himself and her that his imagination must have been working overtime and what he heard must indeed have been a creature of one kind or another. A shudder runs up Lizzy's spine, goosebumps and all. The feeling makes her uncomfortable and a little afraid. "Get a hold of yourself," she thinks," "It was only some little animal who has made a home of the deserted room, for goodness's sake." But instinct tells her that there is more to the incident because she remembers that Kevin didn't say that something walked across the floor; he said SOMEONE walked across the floor, and she is determined to find out what or who it was. With a new shudder of chilling goosebumps, she denounces the eerie feeling and hurries to ready herself for dinner with the family.

At dinner, the adults are anxious to hear about the day's adventures from their two junior detectives and what progress they have to report. Ecstatic at the opportunity to speak of their discoveries, the children take turns relating to the articles, one by one, and of the old soldiers' uniform they uncovered in the first suitcase they selected. However, they did not say anything about the strange, creepy noise that startled Kevin a while earlier. As expected, Hannah, Jessica, and Marshal support the children's exploits and encourage their enthusiasm.

Following dinner, the adults retire to the small library to discuss plans for visiting a few of the House's livestock farms to select pigs and beef cattle for entry in the local Spring Livestock Show.

Lizzy and Kevin meet in the game room to decide which suitcases or trunks they should open next and where and how to store the articles they would like Grandmother Hannah to examine. There may be several items she wants to dispose of, and she is the only one to make that decision. Also, there is always the hope that one of the tightly closed cases may contain the lost key to the other rooms on the third floor.

Lizzy, however, is more interested in drilling her brother about the noise he heard coming from the dark corner of the room upstairs. Of all the pranks he has pulled on her in the past, she recognized the unusual, sudden fear-like surprise in his voice this afternoon. Now it's up to them to discover the source of the footstep-type sound that startled them. Lizzy's instinct tells her not to dismiss the encounter too quickly. Something's amiss, and she intends to find out what it is.

"Time for bed, children." Jessica's soft tone sends the two adventurers up to their rooms, while Dee, who has been fighting drowsiness on the sofa near her mother, begs to be carried to bed. Seeing that her youngest is too exhausted to trust on the stairs alone, she quietly cradles the child, delivers her to the upstairs nursery, and helps her into her Kitty Kat jammies. And like hundreds of times before, Dee is asleep almost before her head reaches the pillow. Jessica sits quietly beside Dee's bed and keeps watch while her baby drifts into the blissful, deep sleep of innocence.

CHAPTER 8:

SINISTER SURPRISE

A muffled thud from overhead wakes a groggy Lizzy who is not sure if she really heard anything at all, or perhaps it was part of a dream which she cannot seems to conjure back into her half-conscious state. She glances at the clock on her nightstand. "Two twenty AM? What on earth woke me up at this hour? It's the middle of the night, for goodness' sake," she mutters crossly. Annoyed and exhausted, she lies back down and credits the disturbance to a bad dream.

Lizzy wakes the next morning with only a slight memory of the noise that jolted her out of bed during the night. Curious, she thinks, as she mentally connects the noise to the sound that startled Kevin the afternoon before. She imagines various excuses for the incident without success and eventually resolves to find a concrete answer during today's search through the storeroom. She is also anxious to find out if her brother woke up from noises about the same time. If both heard it, naturally, it would dismiss the dream theory. And if it wasn't a dream, then something or someone had been in the storeroom with them yesterday and again last night.

Anxious to solve the mystery of last night, she hurries to ready herself for the day. She dresses quickly and starts down the hallway to her brother's room. Halfway there, Kevin emerges and meets her with a look on his face that tells his sister that he, too, had his sleep interrupted in the middle of the night. Shaken, he confronts Lizzy with the same question she intended for him.

"Did you hear the noise from upstairs last night? Would you please tell me I had to be dreaming? It seemed so real; I woke up in a sweat, and I can't seem to forget about it."

"You weren't dreaming, Kevin," Lizzy says in a quiet, comforting tone. She doesn't want to frighten her brother any more than he is. "I heard it too, and we are going to find out who or what it was, right after breakfast. I don't think we should say anything to father or grandmother Hannah unless they mention it first. Their rooms are much further down the hall, and they may not have heard anything. There is no need to concern them with it yet; it might have been just that an animal knocked over some of the things we had stacked up along that one wall. We'll find out when we get up there."

"Lizzy," Kevin says as he leans against the railing at the top of the stairs. "You haven't mentioned the footsteps coming from the room right over mine about half an hour after the first loud thud that came from your direction. I could hear them plain as day."

"Oh, my stars," exclaims Lizzy, obviously caught off guard. She looks surprised at her brother, who is certain now that neither one of them had dreamed about the incident. Agreeing that they must investigate and clear this mystery as soon as possible, they plot to continue their investigation as though nothing had happened.

Following breakfast, the pair of detectives gather their tools, lunches, and what courage they can muster at this time of the morning and head for the third floor to begin the day's adventures. Will they encounter a stowaway, they wonder?

Having agreed earlier that their first task should be to search for evidence of the nocturnal intruder, they enter the storeroom cautiously. Being the eldest, Lizzy enters first, just in case she needs to defend her younger brother against the unknown terror lurking somewhere on this vast floor. For the first time, she realizes that she's scared. Not terrified, but scared just the same.

"Give me your flashlight Kevin," she snaps sharply. "We have to have light; I can hardly see a thing."

"Just a minute," Keven snaps back. "It's probably at the bottom of my sack. Where is your flashlight anyway? You knew it would be dark up here."

Lights, Lizzy says to herself, got to have lights; where's that doggone light switch anyway, she thinks as she realizes that the pounding in her ears is her heartbeat. Groping for the control switch that she knows has to be on the right side of the doorway, she finally feels the familiar metal switch plate and pushes the top button to reveal some of the room's contents. After the pitch-black darkness, even the few dim electric lights are most welcome. While their eyes adjust, the two intrepid investigators stare into the dark corners of the large room, gratified to find no monsters lurking behind the cobwebs or under the thick, century-old dust.

Kevin walks around to the other side of the wall that partially divides the storeroom in two. He examines the area where unopened luggage and boxes remain, waiting to be inspected and tagged.

"Kevin, quick"! Lizzy shouts as Kevin spins around in time to catch the startled look on his sister's face while she backs away from the work area where they spent most of yesterday. At first, he thinks she might faint before reaching her, as he rushes to see what she is staring at that frightens her.

"Lizzy, what is it? Are you alright"? He asks as he reaches her side. Then his eyes follow the pointed finger of her outstretched hand and gasps at the sight before them. His thoughts searched the memories of the day before. It can't be, he reasoned; we were careful to straighten everything up before leaving yesterday.

"Who would have done such a thing, Lizzy?" asks Kevin as he begins to clear a narrow path through the piles of clothing, old tin-type photos, baby dolls, and various other personal belongings from the last century.

As the shock begins to wear off and it becomes apparent that the children are alone in the storeroom, they slowly walk back into the area to assess the damage. It's not as bad as they initially thought. Still, they are upset by the sight of the many large cardboard boxes, suitcases, and steamer trunks torn open and their contents dumped onto the floor as though someone had been desperately searching for something.

"This must be the source of the noises we heard last night," Lizzy surmises. "That large, empty suitcase next to my desk could have dropped and caused the loud thud that woke me up. It's big enough, and judging by the apparent amount of its contents on the floor, it would have been cumbersome.

"Look there," Kevin exclaimed loudly while pointing to the one large trunk that Lizzy uses for her desk. On top of the desk lies a young girl's pink dress and white pinafore, deliberately folded and displayed with great care. On top of the dress, somebody placed one white footman's glove just as carefully as the girls' garments.

CHAPTER 9:

THE PINK DRESS

With the strewn items loosely packed back inside the original cases and the area made ready to continue searching for past clues from the past, both children remain a little bewildered but vigilant. Unnerved, yes. Unquestionably, someone is searching for something, and the children don't know yet what that something may be or if the person who rummaged through the boxes and luggage might be dangerous. Is that person living in this house? Lizzy wonders. Could it be one of the kitchen staff or housemaids? Or maybe one of the maintenance staff? After all, grandmother Hannah will understand if one of the workers has a good reason to search through the stored items. "There's no good reason to disrupt everything and scare us half to death, however," Lizzy thinks out loud. "No good reason at all."

Determined that she and Kevin will not be frightened away from their original task, which might be the reason for the intruder's visit, Lizzy resolves to stick it out and face whatever comes. Secretly, she is hoping that the visitor will give up and go away when they see their scare tactic didn't work. Instinctively, Lizzy crosses her fingers on both hands as she mutters a quiet wish.

"What are you thinking about so hard?" asks Kevin. "After last night, I can't shake the creepy feeling I get just being in here, and what are we going to do if whoever it is comes back?"

"Don't think about that now," Lizzy retorts. "Let's not talk ourselves out of what we came here to do. The fact that someone else is looking for something, too, makes it that much more interesting. Don't you want to know what the intruder was trying to find? You like to explore and chase down mysteries, don't you? Well, we've got a real dandy to figure out this time, so pull yourself together."

"Well, what if we run into this character in person?" Kevin asks nervously. "And what if he's mean?"

"What are you worried about?" Lizzy quips. "There's only one of him, but two of us. We can take care of ourselves."

Having given Kevin a little more confidence in their situation, Lizzy directs their attention back to the mystery of the pink dress and other articles arranged on top of the make-shift desk by the intruder. She decides to examine all the pieces that probably belonged to the young girl and place them in the same luggage as the dress and pinafore.

Let me see, Lizzy ponders to herself. The only little girl that grandmother Hannah spoke of was the youngest of the original owners' two daughters, Celeste, whom the family lost in that horrific fire so long ago. The thought sends chills up Lizzy's spine. What a terrifying way to die.

With that thought giving more immediate importance to their task, not to mention the need to identify their intruder, Lizzy proceeds to locate all items that might have been owned or used by a little girl more than a century ago.

The first to catch her attention is a slate chalkboard about seven by ten inches inside an unfinished wood frame, making the item approximately nine by twelve inches in all and writable on both sides. Children used them in class and also for their homework assignments. It reminds Lizzy and Kevin of the large chalkboards that sprawl across an entire wall in the classrooms at school.

The next item is a small, handmade bag with a ribbon at the top for closing. The little pack contains a dozen small flint, stone, and baked clay marbles. Not the glossy glass marbles of today, but they look well used just the same.

Then, Lizzy notices several lovely little dresses that must have belonged to Celeste. It seems a dress for every occasion, and aprons, pinafores, and smocks to keep the pretty wardrobe clean. Some are very elaborate and heavily trimmed, while others are ornate and lavish with embroidery. Lizzy notes the dainty little pantaloons and pantalettes with the dresses to finish a proper young lady's collection.

Placing some of the remaining articles aside, Lizzy retrieves the pretty pink dress and pinafore that the intruder left behind deliberately to get her and her brother's attention. Yes, it must have belonged to Celeste, she thinks. And with that thought comes a feeling of reverence for the items she has been examining, and she instructs Kevin to fold and re-pack the little girl's property carefully. Keeping the pink dress and pinafore aside for the moment, she begins examining its quality, turning the clothing inside out and wondering if any of her clothes could come close to work put into these garments. Everything seems made to last forever, she thinks and blushes at realizing that she might be a little jealous.

Snapping herself back into the present, she carefully folds the pink dress, but as she slides the pinafore closer, she notices the edge of a folded paper inside one of the pockets. Excited by the find, she Calls Kevin to come and see the discovery. Immediately, Kevin drops what he is doing and joins her.

"Oh golly, Lizzy," he exclaims, nearly breathless with excitement. "Hurry up, see what it says."

"Hold on a minute. I don't want to tear it. After all, it's Been in that pocket for over a hundred years. I thought for a second that the intruder might have put it here, but you can see for yourself the paper has turned a little brown. I hope it isn't brittle or tears easily." Lizzy's hands shake with the suspense of the moment as she tries to slowly recover the fragile paper, grasping it lightly between her thumb and forefinger. Gently, she begins to pull it up from the pocket.

"If it starts to feel like it might tear, I'm going to stop, and we will have to cut the pocket open with scissors. But so far, so good." And holding her breath, Lizzy manages to pull the paper clear of the pocket. "Good grief, I'm nervous," she adds and proceeds to try opening the flimsy letter.

Fortunately, having been stored in a suitcase and deprived of air for the last century, the paper yields a little easier than expected. Lizzy gently smooths it out flat and sends Kevin to the far end of the room to get two spare window panes. Having cleaned the panes, Lizzy carefully placed the letter between them, making it possible to read without fear of damage.

Lizzy reads the letter to Kevin. "My name is Angela Stuart. You found this letter in the pocket of a pinafore belonging to my sister Celeste, who died in a fire along with sixty guests. The fire destroyed most of the third floor of our home, which we have reconstructed. All rooms were locked and remain locked except for this storeroom and one other.

You will think me insane, but I have heard my sister and the guests speak behind closed doors. Somewhere in this house, a key will unlock all of the doors and set them free to leave their third-floor confinement and return home, wherever home is for them. It must be the original key. Please, for the love of God, find that key. I am forbidden ever to mention the subject again. I found the clue below but have been unsuccessful in my search."

The clue continues, "Though some have tried and all did fail, I know that you are smarter. Begin at the bottom, set your sights high, watch your step; you can't go any farther. Focus behind for what you're hoping to find."

CHAPTER 10:

THE PLAN

Grateful for an uninterrupted night's sleep, the two mini-detectives meet after breakfast to plan their strategy for the day. They must begin their search for the original room key in earnest, and judging by the tone of Angela's letter, help can't come any too soon. Unless something has happened in the last One Hundred and Forty-Seven years to change the situation drastically, the lost souls she wrote about remain confined behind those locked doors above. Keeping in mind that someone else in the house is also desperate to locate the key, the children must design a recovery plan of their own.

"The problem is, we can't tell anyone about it," Lizzy confides. "Who would believe us? No one else saw or heard the things we did, and because we are children, they will laugh at us and insist it is all in our imaginations." Lizzy's frustration is noticeable as she struggles to make sense of the last few days' events. A heavy burden for a Pre-teen to bear.

"Well, as I see it, our priorities are clear," she states. "We must find that key. We need it for the victims, and besides, we need it for our original purpose of finding out what, if anything, is stored in those rooms." Lizzy hesitates and then confesses. "I'll tell you what I think, Kevin. I'm certain there are at least two ghosts on the third floor. I believe one is Celeste, and the other is Tucker. I think Tucker is the one who emptied all those suitcases and trunks onto the floor. He's looking for the key! And he's desperate to get out of this house. I believe it was Celeste who laid the dress, pinafore, and glove on the desk for us to find. She knew about the letter and wanted us to find it." Lizzy waits a minute for some reaction from Kevin. Meanwhile, Kevin is almost speechless as he considers the absurdity of what his sister has just told him. Absurd, but how does he argue against what he has seen with his own eyes and heard with his ears?

"Oh, good golly," Kevin blurts out all at once. "This isn't just exploring or solving a simple mystery. It goes beyond anything you and I have ever learned. Good grief, this is serious! What are we going to do, Lizzy? What are we going to do? And I'll tell you something else: Tucker's ghost will not be very friendly if we find the key before he does, and apparently, he's been trying, especially now that he knows someone in the house could find it first." He's frantic and could be dangerous.

"You're right, Kevin. You're right about everything, but what can we do? We have to see it through, or we will never be able to sleep again. We have to know for sure if there is anyone to rescue. Maybe we will find the key and discover that the rooms are empty and Tucker is finally gone. The only way we will know is to find that key and unlock those rooms."

"OK, where do we start?" Kevin asks with a sigh of resolve. Let's get started so we can get it all over with."

"OK, says Lizzy. "let's start with the most obvious. We need to empty what's left of the other crates, luggage, and so on. Let's process everything as quickly as possible while we search each one for the key. Then, we will try to follow the clues in the letter. Write the clues down; we might forget the exact order. We should begin with the first clue - (" Begin at the bottom, set your sights high.") Maybe we need to take the clues literally and start at the bottom by looking on top of things downstairs in the kitchen and food storage rooms. Also, the offices and any other pantries and so forth. I'm guessing, of course, but let's see where it takes us."

"Sounds like a plan," says Kevin, relieved to have a way of unraveling this messy mystery.

"Right, well, be ready to start right after lunch. It will take at least a couple more days to go through the remaining trunks and luggage if there aren't any more interruptions." Lizzy says, determined to solve the puzzle of the missing key.

CHAPTER 11:

THE SECRET SEARCH

At lunch, the two promising detectives try to conceal their concerns and anxiety. However, the adults who want to exhibit support for their children's adventure attempt to show sincere interest in what Lizzy and Kevin have discovered during the long hours up on the third floor of the great house.

Grandmother Hannah is the first to speak up and seems to take the children's exploration as seriously as they do.

"So, tell me, have you found more items that can be used by the town museum or displayed here to interest the tourists? I'm very excited to see all the wonderful things you have exhumed from those old trunks and things. I admit that I took your request to explore at first as playtime for you two, but I can see that it is a very serious hobby, and I applaud the dedication and work you have been putting into it. Also, it makes me happy to see you enjoy this big old house because I worried that you may be unable to find anything here to occupy your time."

"Oh, don't worry, grandmother Hannah," Keven reassures his grandmother. We have plenty to keep us busy," "Lizzy and I have found lots of interesting things in those old boxes. It's kind of like digging for gold, and we still have several cartons and stuff to go through. We plan to go back upstairs after lunch and look for more. By the way, you haven't found an old key lying around somewhere, have you?"

"You mean you are still looking for the original key to the other locked rooms?" Hannah asks, admiring the tenacity of her grandson's question. He's going to make a great lawyer, like his dad, she thinks.

"Yes, ma'am," Kevin replies. "Just thought I would ask."

"No, Kevin, I'm afraid not. But maybe you will still find it in another one of those old trunks." Hannah says encouragingly.

"Don't gulp your food down so fast, children," urges Jessica. "I don't see enough of you two lately, and I enjoy our mealtime together. The things upstairs aren't going anywhere; they will still be there when lunch is over.

"Yes, Ma'am," the children reply. They can read the mild irritation in their mother's voice and feel a little guilty for neglecting her lately.

They finish their lunch quietly and wait to be excused from the table, but Hannah has a surprise for her favorite grandchildren. Mrs. Kelly appears with a three-layer lemon cream cake, a favorite delight she is known for in at least half of Suffolk County. The children's eyes light up with anticipation of the sweet, moist treat. Thoughts of the work waiting upstairs for their attention are distracted by a lemony aroma that permeates the entire room.

"Thank you so much for the delicious cake, grandmother," Lizzy speaks for herself and her brother. "We would like to go downstairs and thank Mrs. Kelly if that's alright.

"Well, I think that is a splendid idea; I'm sure Mrs. Kelly would appreciate that very much," Hannah replies. "Now, go along with you before she and the staff get busy cleaning up and preparing for tonight's dinner."

With their grandmother's blessing, Lizzy and Kevin rush downstairs to see Mrs. Kelly and look around at the areas they will be searching later for the key to estimating the time needed to check each room thoroughly.

Later, as they begin their search "below stairs," as the area is known, they find they can eliminate a few empty rooms.

"Wish we had a map of the rooms so we can keep track," Lizzy thinks out loud. "Wait a minute; I've got an idea. Kevin, go upstairs and find the tourist maps. I think there is a rack in the reception room. If not, look around and see if you can find them. Bring two maps and a couple of pens."

"Sure, Lizzy, that's a great idea; I'll be back in a few minutes," Kevin replies, darting toward the stairwell. Meanwhile, Lizzy continues to search for the elusive key by combing through room after room. She left the doors open to the ones where she would need a step stool to continue.

Kevin returns with the maps and has already grabbed a stool to help with the tall cupboards and pantries. Quickly, Lizzie and Kevin update the maps to avoid unnecessary repetition and continue searching the rooms, pantries, and lockers.

"We must finish down here this afternoon," Lizzy reminds her brother, "then we can go back to the storeroom tomorrow morning to tag the contents of the remaining boxes so grandmother Hannah can decide what she wants to do with everything. It's no problem if she doesn't want to do it right away; we will have already searched everything for the key and hopefully find it by then. Otherwise, it's back to the clues we go, and we can begin on the main floor."

"And let's not forget the North and South wings," suggests Kevin. "They haven't been occupied for some time, but I doubt if the housemaids have time to dust on top of the tall furniture every day."

"Your right," agrees Lizzy. "I nearly forgot all about searching the wings."

The children managed to search the remaining rooms in four hours. Tired and hungry, they return to their rooms in time to wash up and change for supper.

Tapping lightly on his children's doors, Marshal asks them to come quickly and meet at the stairwell.

"I would like us to go down to dinner as a family for a change. Please put everything else aside, and let's enjoy each other's company this evening."

Poor papa, Lizzy ponders. We haven't been spending any time with him or our mother lately. I hope we haven't hurt their feelings. She rushes into the hallway to meet her parents, with Kevin just a few steps behind. Tonight, they will finish a great meal with more of that delicious lemon cream cake and plenty of chatter and laughter among the family.

Lizzy and Kevin have agreed to remain quiet about the intruder and the second visitor who led them to the letter. Their parents would be afraid for the pairs' safety and bring the exploration search to a halt. Who could blame them? It all sounds so impossible and exaggerated. Also, no doubt their father would launch an examination of the house and grounds with men from his staff for the intruders they would never find, and in all, it would just cause the grownups more worry.

Tomorrow, the detectives will split up. Kevin will continue tagging the items in the unopened cartons and then join Lizzy's search of the main floor. Lizzy feels a new excitement about the hunt, though she can't exactly explain why.

'Maybe you've got what mother calls woman's intuition," Kevin says teasingly. "But that can't be it," he continues, "because you're only twelve years old. "Well, we will find out tomorrow." He snickers.

"Alright, children, time for bed. I hope you can sleep well after all of the food you put away tonight," teases Jessica. "Now upstairs you go; I'll be in to say goodnight soon."

Later, having already said her prayers and comfy in her favorite pajamas, a very sleepy Lizzy snuggles down into bed, knowing it won't be long before she is fast asleep for the night. She has no way of knowing at the time, but her comfort is about to be interrupted by a face-to-face meeting she isn't expecting.

CHAPTER 12:

INTRUDER ALERT

Lizzy wakes a little after midnight. Noises are coming from the room above. Unnerving noises that are not only disturbing but infuriating, especially at this time of night. Undoubtedly, it can only mean the intruder is back, so it's time to challenge the visitor.

Lizzy concentrates intently on the sounds. Some of them are raspy, like the sound of wooden boxes being dragged a few feet along the wood floor. Another sound is creaking wood planks or lids giving way under pressure as she imagines someone prying the crates open right above her.

Whoever it is, she thinks, needs to be found out. Nervous but unafraid, Lizzy is determined to find out who the intruder is for sure.

But what if it is Tucker's ghost? Lizzy asks herself, squirming at the thought while she reaches for her robe. How does a person approach a spirit? Goodness me, ghosts aren't real; they can't hurt anyone! I'll wake Kevin up, and we will go up there and stop this nonsense.

Lizzy grabs her flashlight, puts a candle and some matches in her robe pocket, just in case, and quietly but quickly walks to her brother's room.

"Wake up, Kevin," Lizzy whispers as she shakes Kevin by the shoulder. "Wake up. There's someone upstairs in the storeroom, and we're going up to find out who it is. Get up, put on your robe, and don't forget your flashlight."

"Are you crazy, Lizzy?" Kevin replies, rubbing the sleep from his eyes. "What do you think you're going to do? It sounds dangerous to me. Go back to bed."

"No," Lizzy states emphatically. "We are going up there and stop whoever it is. We can threaten to turn them over to the police if we have to. Either way, we're going to confront this doggone intruder! Now come on, enough is enough."

"Aw, okay," Kevin relents. "But I still think it's too dangerous."

Still groggy from lack of sleep, the two fearless mini-detectives climb the stairs to the third floor. Flashlights in hand, they reach the upstairs hallway. They had forgotten how pitch black it gets up here where the night hides everything, especially the light switch at the far end of the hall. In front of them, the flashlights provide just enough light to see the path before them, but as Kevin glances backward, it is impossible to see past the wall of darkness behind them. His knees weaken as he begins to realize how vulnerable he and his sister are at this moment, knowing that there is someone else up here who may be a ghost or a killer. As the two finally reach the switch, he struggles to overcome his imagination and is relieved to find that the control still works.

The lighting is still very dim, but enough to make out the storeroom door. Before entering, the two children stand very still and listen keenly for any sound coming from inside. They hear nothing but the sounds of their breathing, so getting a grip on their nerves, Lizzy opens the door and reaches to the right for the switch as they enter. But just as she is about to push the button, they hear a gruff, throaty voice from inside the darkness.

"Come on in, children," the deep, husky voice invites. "Come on in and close the door." Lizzy and Kevin remain frozen at the room entrance, unable to move until, in uncanny unison, they shine their lights in the direction of the gravelly voice.

"Oh my Gosh," Lizzy utters, half under her breath. Still frozen with fear, Kevin reaches for Lizzy's hand and holds it as if his life depends on it; at this moment, he may be right. Both children stand perfectly still, afraid their movement may cause this ghastly phantom-like creature to lunge toward them.

Now Lizzy, assessing her fear, wonders if she is brave enough to drag her brother and run for the stairwell. Not sure of herself, she remains where she is and holds Kevin close to comfort him as he sobs with fright.

Unlike anything in her imagination, the creature stands before them in grotesque reality, and Lizzy begins to doubt her sanity. It can't be, she thinks, but she cannot make the vision go away. She stares at the half-human, half-ghost-like thing in front of her, partially hidden by the darkness. A hideous image of a man having been disfigured, twisted in agony, engulfed by flames as he helplessly burned alive.

"Oh, Golly," Lizzy exclaims as she recognizes what she thinks is part of a footman's uniform clinging to the wretched form before her. "You're Tucker"! "What on earth do you want of us?"

"Congratulations, Miss Elizabeth. How did you know it was me? The phantom answers in a condescending voice. The rumors around town, or the stories saved to tell the tourists? I want the original key, and you must have it by now. I have to have it to leave this house, and I'm going to get it, one way or another, and I don't care what I have to do. Give it to me, now," his voice thunders angrily as he takes a few threatening steps toward the children.

Quickly, Lizzy punches the button on the light switch, hoping to make the horrid creature cringe from the additional lighting. The sight takes her breath away as the gargoyle-like apparition looms over her and her brother. Never before have they been so terrified. He's a nightmare, she realizes. A walking, talking, hideous monster! His eyes look hollow but have glowing, blood-red centers in the face of burnt flesh.

"We don't have the key," Lizzy stammers. We have been looking for it but haven't found it yet, honest. She's shaking uncontrollably, almost sure that this ferocious beast intends to kill, if necessary, to get what he wants. "Why do you need the key to leave? Can't you go and leave us in peace? I don't understand."

"You're testing my patience, little girl, the mangled form warns. I won't hesitate to torture you and your little brother until I get that key. Remember, I have nothing to lose."

Lizzy senses growing anger and impatience from the creature and needs to buy time so she and Kevin can get away. She tries to reason with Tucker.

"You haven't answered my question, Tucker. I want to understand, but I can't until you tell me why you need the key. I see no reason you shouldn't have it, and we only want to find it so we can open all the other rooms up here. The doors have stayed locked all this time, and we are just curious. Won't you please tell us more? I promise we will continue to help you look for the key."

"Are you toying with me, young lady? The monster bellows. Do you think I'm stupid? I'm warning you, Miss Priss, I will deal harshly with the two of you if you provoke me further. You have no use for the original key I seek except to taunt me cruelly. Haven't I suffered enough? One hundred and forty-seven years, I have roamed these rooms—nearly a century and a half of hopelessness without end. Listen well, and remember what I say. I will have that key, or I will have your heads," the demon promises as he picks up an old ax and slings it across the room to bury the blade in the far wall next to the window.

Lizzy and Kevin cringe as the heavy weapon vibrates from the impact. Still confused by part of Tucker's statement, she feels compelled to try for an explanation. "Tucker, I told you the truth; we only want the key to open the other doors with honestly. Why is that so wrong?"

"Could it be that the answer hasn't occurred to you?" Tucker asks. "Then answer me this, young lady. What makes you think the old key would open the new doors or haven't you asked yourself that question yet? "

"New doors?" Repeats Lizzy. "Oh, Golly. Of course, I get it now. Oh, how could I have been so dumb?" forgetting her fear and realizing her obvious blunder, she backtracks mentally to align the facts and rethink the situation. "The doors were replaced after the fire because nearly all rooms had more smoke damage than anything, but the doors burned before the fire department arrived. Therefore, the new doors have a new key. Oh, for goodness sake, there are two keys for this floor, and both are missing. " Lizzy slouches in unbelief, almost falling to the floor. "Okay, Tucker, then why do you need the original key if there are none of the original doors to open?"

"Now you're catching on, girlie," Tucker replies, his voice a little less threatening now, as though realizing the misunderstanding. "You can open the new doors with the new key, but only the original key will open the portal to the past and release all of us from that period so long ago and allow us to return to where we belong."

With a few words between themselves, the children reach a limited understanding of Tucker's circumstances, prompting an almost sympathetic response. Trusting her instincts, a shaky but determined Lizzy attempts to reason with Tucker. After all, she says to herself, things can't get much worse.

"Tucker, please listen to what we have to say, and for goodness sake, don't get angry," Lizzy pleads.

At First, Tucker is annoyed at the audacity of his bold, young captives, but then he slowly steps back a few paces to signal his willingness to do as they ask.

"Look," Lizzy begins, "Kevin and I don't think you want to harm us. After all, you wouldn't have suffered if you had not returned to the fire to save Miss Celeste. We are beginning to recognize your predicament and how limited you are to do anything about it. What if we work together somehow? Kevin and I want to find the new key anyway, so there is no reason not to look for them both. The search could go a lot faster if you help."

"Help you; how can I help you when I can't leave the third floor?" Tucker replies with desperation in his voice. "The wretched thing I did has cursed me and the others with confinement here and no hope unless we have the key to the portal."

"Trust me, Tucker." The twelve-year-old pleads as she takes a few steps toward the creature to show her good intentions. "Think hard; remember as much as you possibly can about where the keys might be. Who kept the keys? Was it the housekeeper or some other member of staff? Would they be on a key ring or hanging on a hook somewhere? Try Tucker, try very hard. Also, here is a copy of the clue we found that Angela wrote Celeste's sister. Maybe you can figure out the riddle; Keven and I haven't been able to yet."

"You won't betray me to your family, will You?" Tucker asks, with a warning in his tone.

"No, we won't say a word about you," Lizzy promises, with Kevin standing shyly by her side, shaking his head in agreement. "They wouldn't believe us anyway." She teases. "Okay, it's agreed. Kevin and I will continue searching in the morning. If you need to talk to us, "She says as she removes her blue hair ribbon, "tie this ribbon around the banister at the top of the stairs, and I'll come up after everyone else is asleep."

Tucker agrees, and taking the hair ribbon, he disappears into the night. Breathing an enormous sigh of relief, the two sleepy detectives light their way back to their rooms with much to consider.

CHAPTER 13:

RESUMING THE SEARCH

At breakfast, bright-eyed and well-rested, Lizzy and Kevin look forward to resuming the search with new enthusiasm. Using a type of sign language that all children develop to prevent parents from knowing what they're up to, these juvenile investigators secretly arrange their day. Grandmother Hannah chuckles, watching little Dee's head swing side to side, trying to follow the silent conversation of her siblings.

Everyone seems to have a busy day planned, which means less interference for Kevin and Lizzy's searches. Kevin will continue tagging items on the third floor as planned. Still, Lizzy will attempt to hunt through everything on the main floor, an enormous undertaking in a house this size.

Marshal will oversee the seeding of spring crops for a timely fall harvest and preventive maintenance of estate structures while Hannah and Jessica are settling the plans to prepare the manor for the first tourist invasion of the year.

Lizzy chooses to begin her search in the extensive library, which is also the perfect setting for her father's office. For as long as she can recall, his massive desk has been surrounded by hundreds of books. The only difference in the current subject matter compared to the older titles of the manors' library is that Marshal's collection pertains to the study, application, and execution of state and federal corporate law. According to her father, the most valuable to him is the seventy hard-bound volumes citing case studies he often refers to.

Lizzy is impressed by the overwhelming amount of knowledge contained in this one great room. She wants to launch the task at hand but estimates that examining each shelf of books in the three ceiling-to-floor wall fixtures would take as many days to complete. She decides to continue with the rest of the rooms and save this mammoth undertaking for last, knowing the possibility that the key may turn up somewhere else on this floor.

She moves to the small library, where she is fascinated with the comfort-purpose features of the room, like the pale blue, overstuffed sofa and chairs with matching footstools. Small wooden tables of hand-rubbed mahogany stand ready with individual silver cigarette tins, crystal ashtrays, and monogrammed beverage coasters. With slightly more than two hundred books and magazines available, the quiet room is the perfect place to enjoy reading the classics or choose lighter material for entertainment.

Utilizing the shorter of the two library ladders, Lizzy examines the bookshelves, wall hangings, and surfaces of fixtures and cabinets around the room but fails to find the elusive keys.

Next to inspect is the formal dining room, and the number of possible hiding places is many. Upon entering, the grand, stately room dominates the senses with the manor's history of visiting royalty and promises of the uttermost in refined dining pleasure. As usual, Lizzy is in awe of the extravagance on display with genuine pride. The long dark wooden table, polished and elegantly appointed with delicate lace doilies, will seat thirty easily. Gleaming silver candelabras sit at both ends, with an elegant crystal vase of fresh flowers adorning the center, matching sideboards, buffet, and beverage bar of equal beauty stand waiting while a magnificent crystal chandelier lights the room where a collection of original portraits and depictions of past Stuart masters, their families, U.S.presidents, and other dignitaries line the walls.

Putting her thoughts of the charm and beauty of her environment aside, Lizzy carefully checks every piece of furniture's crack and crevice. Finding nothing, she selects the taller ladder this time to access the portraits and other wall hangings, which are hung much higher in this room and the formal living room for better viewing.

She meticulously inspects each canvass and frame for the rest of the afternoon at this task. Discouraged and frustrated, Lizzy must abandon her project for the day with only thirty minutes to clean up and change for dinner. She is anxious to meet with Kevin afterward, although she knows he would have come downstairs and told her immediately if he had found anything. Tomorrow, she will resume her search in the informal dining-breakfast room, which is smaller and will allow time to begin in the large formal living room and foyer.

During dinner, the pair of tired junior detectives agree to spend the evening with the adults for a change. Jessica and Marshal will cherish the additional time with the children, and in turn, the sister and brother team will enjoy some much-needed parental pampering.

Before joining the adults, Kevin reports to his sister that he has heard voices while in the storeroom tagging the belongings left behind by the old residents.

"It's bizarre; the sounds seem to be coming from the other locked rooms, but not loud enough to understand. And I haven't seen or heard from Tucker again", Kevin tells his sister in a nervous tone, "but I often feel he is in the room. Maybe he is watching me from somewhere else, but it sure reminds me that we must find the keys before he loses his patience."

"Don't worry," answers Lizzy. "He knows what we are trying to do, and he also knows he can't do it alone as long as he can't come down to the other floors. I wish we could figure out Angela's clues. Things would move along more quickly. "Begin at the bottom, set your sights high…." I can't make sense of it. We started at the bottom level, and I checked everything in the rooms, including all the paintings and souvenirs up high. What else could it mean?"

"It beats me," Kevin responds. "The answer is probably something simple, and we are going to feel so stupid for not catching on all this time."

"I'm already feeling kind of brainless," Lizzy sighs. "Let's go find mom and grandmother Hannah, and don't forget to watch what you say," she cautions her brother. "They mustn't guess our secret, or there will be no end to the trouble it will cause."

CHAPTER 14:

CHANGING THE RULES

The informal dining and breakfast room is a cozy, family favorite place to enjoy. While still lavish and exciting, it is the least demanding of cultural deportment. In this private dining room, proper behavior is minding one's "P's" and "Q's," and no one is likely to be sent to the proverbial "tower" for using the wrong fork at dinner. Likewise, if the three Stuart children had their way, every meal would include "finger food."

Lizzy feels optimistic about the morning search, though still wrestling with the brain-twisting riddle in Angela's note. She knows she must get her mind off the question of why the clue had to be a riddle and concentrate on the instructions described on the paper.

Tackling her primary task for the day, she begins her two-hour scan of the rooms' furnishings, cabinets, closets, and other fixtures. Saving the antique souvenirs and paintings for last, she maneuvers the small ladder around the room, carefully checking every article to complete the job, knowing she has left nothing to chance.

Sightly apprehensive but not deterred, Lizzy enters the formal living room. Somewhat intimidated by the size and splendor of the great room, Lizzy takes her first honest look, absorbing the character and distinction found only in this room and the formal reception area that adjoins the main foyer. Through her mind's eye, she can imagine how it must have been so long ago. The President of the United States and, likewise, foreign presidents and other dignitaries were welcomed by the Stuart family here. With them, the grand ladies of that period were adorned in gowns and jewels reflecting their status. Prominent families of Boston called at Stuart Manor regularly to secure a favored place in early nineteen hundred society.

51

Snapping herself back into the present, Lizzy initiates her search by mentally dividing the rooms into three parts to keep her search organized. She will begin at the north end of the room nearest the exit leading to the formal dining room and work forward toward the main entrance and reception area. Knowing that just the living room itself will be an all-day project, she wastes no time by starting immediately. At lunchtime, Kevin draws his sister aside with a message from Tucker.

"Tucker caught me by surprise a couple of hours ago. He's becoming impatient and wants to know how far along you are with the search. He said to look for the hair ribbon on the staircase railing tonight on our way to our rooms. He wants to talk to us."

"Oh, great," sighs Lizzy. "A full, boring day of moving things around, climbing up and down ladders, and searching every crack and crevice for two small keys, and our resident ghoul wants a meeting." Kevin giggles at his sister's reference to Tucker, though her description is correct. Ghoul, ghost, bogeyman, doesn't matter, she's right, he tells himself.

"Well, Liz, we must go see him, or he will keep us up all night and might wake the others," Kevin answers. "Anyway, I don't trust him. He gives me the creeps."

"Sure," she replies. "We don't have a choice. Maybe we can get a little extra sleep if we go to bed right after dinner. I'll set my alarm for about 1:30 a.m. Everyone should be asleep by then."

Groggy and annoyed, Lizzy silences the noisy alarm and forces herself onto her feet. She opens a window, inviting the cool breeze to help clear her head while taking a few deep breaths to relieve herself of the urge to lie back down. "Why can't that stupid ghost meet us in the daytime," she mumbles. Grabbing her robe and flashlight, she walks silently down the hall to her brothers' room. Kevin, already about half awake, is wrestling with the robe he accidentally put on inside out.

"Hurry up, Kevin," his sister urges. "Let's get this over with so we can go back to bed."

"You're amazing sis. We are going upstairs to meet with an enormous, dangerous, not to mention a hideous thing with a voice,

52

and you treat the situation like a mild irritation to your busy day," Kevin stammers. "Okay, so I'm afraid of this Tucker creature. I won't deny it."

"So, who isn't scared?" Lizzy replies sharply. "The weaker he thinks we are, the more demanding he will become. We have the advantage if he wants to leave this house. We have to use that advantage, and that's why I'm going to insist he meet us during the daylight hours. Just because he no longer needs his sleep doesn't mean we can't get ours. Mom, Dad, and Grandmother Hannah are used to us going to the third floor during the day, and they know we are looking for the door key. "You've got the point there," Kevin replies.

"Tonight, we make the rules, "Lizzy says with a smile as the pair reaches the stairway. One step at a time and into the darkness, the flashlights provide little comfort when they remember the malformed, freakish sight that awaits them. It's one of those things you can't unsee.

When they reach the closed door of the storeroom, the dim lights and movement of colors coming from underneath the door tell them that Tucker is already in the room and waiting. Lizzy opens the door and immediately reaches for the light switch to her right, taking a deep breath. A hideous laugh greets them as Tucker is well aware of their initial fright and uses it to intimidate them. A maneuver that Lizzy anticipated.

"Don't bother with all your scare tactics this time, Tucker, because you and I both know you don't intend to carry through with your threats, that is, if you still want help finding those keys," Lizzy scolds.

The apparition begins to change in size. The laughter screams louder as the phantasm grows larger, changing to swirling colors of red, blue, and purple. At the same time, a wind violently blows inside the storeroom, shredding old curtains from the windows and making it difficult for the children to stand.

"You dare to make demands, you little insignificant pipsqueak. Don't you know I can squash you like a bug with just one blow or tear you limb from limb for being so impertinent?" Doors and windows rattle as the voice thunders. The terrified youngsters expect lightning

53

to strike inside the room at any moment. But Lizzy knows that if she and her brother give in to this ranting monster, he will have them under his thumb from now on. So, she gathers all of her courage and screams back with all her might.

"And furthermore, there will be no more meetings in the middle of the night. We need our sleep even if you don't, so we meet during the daytime from now on. Now, if you want to go on playing bogeyman, then we are going back downstairs, and when we find the keys, we will keep them to ourselves."

Surprised at the young girl's courage, Tucker slowly reduces his tantrum and returns to the phantom image the children remember. "Why do you think you have the right to make the rules?" he asks in his usual gruff voice.

"We have the right because you are the one who caused this problem. You are responsible for the fire that killed those innocent people that night," Lizzy answers. "So, from now on, either work with us without shenanigans or leave us alone and forget about the keys."

CHAPTER 15:

ELUSIVE KEYS

Before leaving the late-night meeting, Lizzy and Kevin finished making their position clear and demanded that Tucker have more input. Lizzy made him promise to at least make a reasonable effort to help solve the riddle and to give her information on those poor souls confined in the other rooms. What will she discover when they finally have the keys?

"Anything you can remember about the person who handled the keys," Lizzy had said before the two left the floor to go back to bed, feeling confident they had successfully turned the tables and taken control away from Tucker at last.

Spring sunshine, a warm breeze through the open windows, and birds' comforting sounds greet the children the following day. Lizzy and Kevin have slept in for only the second time since moving into the great house. It feels good, and they meet downstairs in the breakfast room to find that everyone else has already eaten and begun their tasks for the day. But Mrs. Kelly has been listening for the sleepy pair and has kept their favorite breakfast foods hot.

Kevin has only one more crate in the storeroom to pry open and tag the contents, so he agrees to join his sister on the main floor afterward. Splitting the remaining search will make the work go faster.

Lizzy finishes the remainder of the formal living room in just three hours and moves on to the reception area. The room is a massive, plush section of the manor but with fewer places to hide the keys. Black and white photographs of many dignitaries are displayed on the walls and in ornate picture frames placed strategically on furniture pieces around the room, including photos of the first all-talking movie titled "Lights of New York" in 1928. Movie stars Helene Costello, Cullen Landis, and Eugene Palette donated signed copies of their photos to the Stuart family. Naturally, these treasures are placed far behind rope barriers during tourist visits.

After finishing the reception area in just two hours, Lizzy rests on an overstuffed sofa for a while. She imagines what it must have been like to have celebrities coming and going almost regularly. Some came for dinner and an evening's entertainment, while others took advantage of Stuart's hospitality to escape the crowds and demands of public life. One of the manor's cottages would be made available if they were after solitude. For example, in 1905, President Theodore Roosevelt Jr. Occupied the south wing of the estate for four days. His security team occupied four second-floor bedrooms while rotating their duties to guard the wing and grounds. His abbreviated office and kitchen staff occupied bedrooms below ground.

Lizzy thinks how grand it must have all been, and realizing she has been daydreaming for almost half an hour, she gets up from the comfortable sofa to continue searching the main entrance and long hallway. But before she can reach the pair of ornate entry doors, she sees Kevin coming down the stairs. She assumes he has finally finished in the storeroom.

"It's all done, Lizzy. Everything has been tagged and arranged for Grandmother Hannah. I think she will want to use most of it here in the house for the tourists to see," Kevin announces joyfully. "How can I help you down here?"

"You can help here in the entranceway," Lizzy replies. "check every place where keys can be hidden. Meanwhile, I'll get the tall ladder and start in the hallway." By the way, did you hear voices coming from the other rooms again today?

"Oh yes, I meant to tell you about that. Yes, I did hear some people speaking, but I can never make out what they are saying. But get this," Kevin says excitedly, "today, I know I heard music coming from the room closest to where I was working. Very faint, but I knew it was music I had never heard before. I'm sure it was what people danced to in the olden days. I'm guessing it was a waltz."

"Oh my gosh," Lizzy responds. "This gets stranger by the minute. Dance music? How in the world would ghosts dance the waltz?" She has a mental picture of sixty ghosts, as hideous as Tucker, paired up and dancing to music in a locked room on the third floor. "What a horrid thought," she exclaims. "That can't be possible. But then I didn't think Tucker was possible either." She continues to question her brother. "Did you see Tucker today?"

"No, I didn't see him or hear him around today," replies Kevin. "If I had, I would have asked him about the music."

"Well, for goodness sake," Lizzy says with a sigh. "I would sure like to hear what he has to say about the music. I think I'll tie a ribbon of my own to the railing tonight, and we can try to see him tomorrow morning. We need some answers."

Dropping the conversation, the team continues their searches for the mysterious keys. Kevin finishes the entrance and helps his sister finish the long hallway in time to wash up for dinner.

Later that evening, Lizzy ties one of her pink ribbons to the top railing on the third floor with a short note to meet after breakfast the following day. She and her brother have decided to get as much information as Tucker can give them about the other victims and concentrate on Angela's note. Searching the rooms takes so long, and they can always return to that if they can't solve the riddle. It's worth a try.

CHAPTER 16:

RHYME OR REASON

The following day, Lizzy and her brother are in the third-floor storeroom waiting for Tucker.

"You did a great job up here, Kevin," Lizzy says with pride. He has categorized and tagged everything so well for a boy who will be just ten years old soon. "Grandmother Hannah will have no trouble separating items to use for the tourists and those she will be taking to the museum for display. I'm proud of you."

Kevin grins from ear to ear at the unexpected praise. "Aw, thanks, it was fun. Except for running into Tucker."

"Did I hear my name mentioned?" Tucker's gruff voice interrupts. "Why are we meeting this morning? Have you found the keys?"

"No, Tucker, we haven't found the keys," Lizzy retorts," and I really wish you would find a way to cover yourself up. I mean, you are a horrible sight first thing in the morning, you know. I'm sorry, but if you want us to consider you a friend, please try not to look so frightening all the time. Surely you can understand what it's like for us. Maybe we will find the keys if we can solve the doggone riddle in Angela's note between the three of us. Right now, that's our best chance of any progress. Tucker, you know this house better than we do; surely the riddle gives you some clue. Let's concentrate on the instructions she left. We should take them one at a time and discuss the possibilities."

Kevin speaks up first. "Okay, at this point, we have nothing to lose. Let's give it a try. So, the first clue says in part, "...Begin at the bottom...".

Lizzy interrupts. "So, we need to know, the bottom of what? It can't be the bottom of the house; we have searched everything down there and half of the main floor besides. And it can't mean another building because it wouldn't fit either."

"The servants always come up from the underground rooms by way of the servant's stairs," Tucker remarks. "Did you check those stairs for the keys?"

"No, I forgot about those stairs," Lizzy responds. "Good thinking, I'll check them first thing after lunch. Okay, now what else? The bottom of what?"

Kevin gets his sister's attention and reminds her, "Well, Lizzy, we haven't checked the stairs going up from the main hall yet, either."

"Kevin, that's it," shrieks Lizzy. "That's it! The bottom of the stairs! Oh my gosh, that has to be what the riddle meant." Lizzy squeezes her brother with a big hug as he squirms to catch his breath.

"Okay, but which stairs," Tucker asks excitedly.

"Both," Lizzy responds. "We will check the servants' stairs first and then the main stairway. It depends on the next part of the riddle, too. It says, "...Begin at the bottom, set your sights high...", so we need to figure out what that second part means. Can it simply mean "high," as in the landing at the top of the stairway? I'll try it this afternoon with the servant's stairs. I was going to check them anyway."

"I'll go with you," says Kevin eagerly. "I can hardly wait to get started and see where the riddle takes us."

"I can't believe we may find those keys today or tomorrow," adds Tucker. "There is no stopping now; we are too close."

"It's been a long, long time for you, Tucker," Lizzy comments in a sympathetic tone. "I can only imagine what it has been like all this time. We're not giving up until we find those keys."

"Okay, Lizzy, let's go downstairs and get ready. We can start the servants' stairs as soon as lunch is over," Kevin interjects impatiently, "I can hardly wait; I'm sure we're on the right track."

"Hold on, settle down," Lizzy demands, with one hand against Kevin's chest. "You're wound up tighter than a fifty-cent watch. We can't just get up from the table and begin searching. We must wait at least thirty minutes. The maids will be clearing the table so that staff will go up and down those stairs, and we can't show a good reason for being in their way. We can only check that area between the time they finish their duties for one meal and begin making the room ready for the next."

"Oh, I didn't think of that," replies Kevin, embarrassed by his overzealous display. "You're right, of course; we don't want them asking questions we can't answer."

Lizzy estimates that staff will be using the stairs in about ninety minutes, preparing the small dining room for lunch. She and Kevin decide to begin their search at the bottom of the servants' stairway and work as far us as they can with the time they have left. Fortunately, the inspection from the kitchen to the dining room was completed quickly. They encountered no staff to wonder why the pair were not using the main stairs instead of the cramped servants' stairway.

"Now we have two sets of stairs to check from here. Which should we do first, Lizzy?" Kevin asks."

"I don't think we should tackle the servants' stairs until about thirty to forty-five minutes after lunch, so we may as well begin with the main staircase to the second floor. We can begin there now, break for lunch, and continue right after. Don't forget we must check around the carpeting on the steps and look on top and behind the paintings as we go."

"Oh, and we almost forgot to look in the big closet under the main staircase. Let's start there," Kevin suggests.

"Good idea," Lizzy answers approvingly. "You're becoming quite a detective! But first, go there and check to see if the closet is locked. If it is, we will have to get the key from Mrs. Kelly, or find the head housemaid, though I don't know what excuse we can give for needing it."

Kevin runs down the hallway to the staircase closet and, holding his breath, attempts to turn the knob. The door opens with little effort, and Kevin breathes a big sigh of relief. He motions to Lizzy that the coast is clear as he pulls the string to the closet light.

Together, the pair of young sleuths check the area thoroughly, grateful to Mrs. Kelly for keeping the closets and pantries so well organized. However, no keys are found here either.

"Okay, little brother, let's go to the bottom of the main staircase and see what we can find," urges Lizzy, holding up both hands with fingers crossed.

"Right behind you, sis," Kevin replies confidently. "I know; we are close to finding those keys. Don't ask me how I know, but I'm sure of it."

"Well then," encourages Lizzy. "This is going to be our lucky afternoon." Both children hurry forward to the stairway, giggling with excitement.

"Kevin, go up to the second-floor landing and look around the floor and carpet edges. The keys are small and thin, so there may be a crack in the wood flooring or a small tear in the carpet somewhere. I'll start here at the bottom and look for the same things. Let's not forget to check these old portraits before we move to the next flight if we don't find anything."

Lizzy and Kevin, confident that they will soon find their target, closely examine every possible crevice and suspicious bump. Once they meet on the second-floor landing empty-handed, they proceed to inspect all five of the large and heavy portraits carefully.

"Well, foiled again," Lizzy sighs, quoting a line she read somewhere in one of her detective stories. "We may as well continue to the top of the third floor."

They are about to begin from the bottom of the last staircase when Lizzy stops. Her eyes become transfixed on the edge of the landing at the top of the thirty-two steps. She doesn't move or speak, and the look on her face tells Kevin that his sister has just had a revelation and is working something out in her mind.

"Good golly, Lizzy. What is it? What are you thinking? You have an idea, don't you?" Her brother begs her to speak and let him in on the mystery.

Finally, Lizzy asks Kevin for his copy of the riddle, which he carries in the pocket of his jeans. "I don't want it; just read it to me slowly," she asks.

Kevin, slightly confounded at his sisters' behavior, begins to read the riddle. "Though some have tried and all did fail, I know that you are smarter. Begin at the bottom, set your sights high, watch your step; you can't go any farther.

"Stop, stop there!" Lizzy demands. She repeats the last four words back to her brother. "You can't go any farther. Kevin, we should have realized the third floor is as far as anyone can go! Don't you see? We are almost there! We need to follow the last instruction of the riddle!"

"You're right, Lizzy," Kevin bellows and begins reading. "Focus behind for what you're hoping to find. Oh golly, let's go up top and see what that last line means."

Immediately, the two climb feverishly to the top and sit down on the landing to catch their breath. Seeing that the pair will need more light, Kevin runs down the hall to the switch at the end to light the entire gallery.

"Focus behind," Lizzy keeps repeating. "Behind what?" still seated on the landing, she gazes down the stairs where the only thing to see are four portraits. The first is of President Jackson, who hired Reginald Stuart as the diplomatic envoy to Great Britain. Lizzy remembers that Reginald was the one who had the great house built back in 1803. The next portrait is of George W. Frederick, King of Great Britain and Ireland. She can't recall who the men are in the remaining two pictures.

"Kevin," Lizzy squeals. "Focus behind for what you're hoping to find." The only things around that we can look behind are these portraits! Quick, let's get the first one down."

"The one of Andrew Jackson?" Kevin asks.

"Yes," confirms Lizzy. "Let's hurry, but don't damage the painting. Golly, I'm getting awful nervous; keep your fingers crossed, this could be it."

Slowly, the children lower the weighty canvas creation and carry it the short distance to the gallery wall. Here, they can turn it around without worry of damage or the possibility that one of them could fall down the stairs.

Leaning the valuable rendition of Jackson against the wall, the two examine the front, thinking that perhaps the keys may be inserted between the thick, elegant frame and the aged canvas. Removing a thick layer of dust, they inspect the hand-carved wood's many small holes and odd shapes. Unfortunately, their careful prodding is unsuccessful, leaving only the backside of the painting as a Possible hiding place in the one painting that fits the riddle's description.

With great care, Lizzy and Kevin maneuver the portrait to turn the front to the wall, allowing only the top edge of the frame to rest against it. Just as the back is in view, Kevin hollers, "Lizzy, we did it," as he reaches for a small burlap pouch hanging from a tiny hook embedded in the top of the frame. Without hesitation, he dumps the contents. Two door keys and a note spill out onto the floor. Kevin squeals with delight. "Woo-hoo, Lizzy, we really did it; we solved the riddle!"

"Golly, I can hardly believe my eyes," exclaims Lizzy breathlessly. "It's over; the search is really over. Now we can find out what is behind the locked doors, and Tucker can return to where he belongs. It's just wonderful!"

"And we can find out where that music has been coming from," screeches Kevin, a full octave higher than usual.

"We need to find Tucker," Lizzy reminds her brother." After all, he and others have suffered for over a century.

"Hey, sis, where is that note that fell out with the keys? Oh, there it is; let's see what it says," Kevin adds as he scoops the paper up from the floor and hands it to Lizzy."

CHAPTER 17:

SHADOWS AND MUSIC

"Golly, I hope it's not another riddle," Lizzy snickers. "We don't need to go through that again." Gingerly, she unfolds the paper and begins to read, "Congratulations, If you are reading this, you have solved the riddle and found the keys. There is only one thing to keep in mind from this point on. These two keys must remain together at all times. Whoever has custody must have both keys. If separated, neither key will work. The question of why remains a mystery. There are rumors that the spirits of the victims haunt this great house, and the key to the doors destroyed by the fire is to be used to release those spirits. We only know that before they located the original key in the rubble, the new master key would not work for the new replacement doors. Therefore, to keep the rooms locked from this day forward, both keys remain together and hidden from the past. What happens to them in the future is your responsibility.

"Uh-oh," Kevin says quietly.

"What do you mean by that?" Lizzy barks

"I mean, it looks like we are going to have big trouble with Tucker," Kevin snaps back. "He expects us to give him the old key for the so-called "portal." But we can't give it to him because the new key would be useless."

"Good grief," mutters Lizzy. "I see what you mean. Well, maybe there is a way that we can use it to send him back where he came from."

"We better hope so," Kevin sighs. "Or else there's no way of knowing what he will do, and I don't know how we can stop him."

Pocketing the pouch with its precious contents, Lizzy and her brother replaced the portrait on the wall and returned to the main floor in time for lunch. They agree that it would be better not to mention the keys to the family until they can explain Tucker and the rest of the mystery behind Stuart Manor.

Tired of searches and riddles, exploring the locked rooms will have to wait until tomorrow morning as the children decide to spend the rest of the day with family. It has been a big day for these pint-sized investigators, and now it's time to wind down and relax with those they love.

Early the following day, Marshal and his mother find their two sleuth hounds at the breakfast table, hurriedly feasting on French toast drenched in butter, powdered sugar, and syrup.

"Good heavens," Hannah exclaims. "Slow down before you make yourself sick. The food isn't going anywhere; we won't run out of anything before your tummies are full," she teases.

"We're sorry, Grandmother," Lizzy apologizes for herself and her brother. Kevin glances sheepishly in his father's direction to see if he is angry with their conduct and is relieved to see an understanding smile instead.

With stomachs pleasantly full, the brother and sister team excuse themselves from the table and dash to the third floor and the adventures that await them.

Lizzy's hand quivers with anticipation, standing outside the first locked door as she inserts the newer key into the lock. She stops to take a big breath before turning the key. "Oh my stars," she says as her complexion flushes bright pink. "Silly, isn't it?" she remarks to her brother. "All of a sudden, I don't feel so good."

"Hey," Kevin replies. "It's only nerves. You're just too excited after the big breakfast we had. After all, this is the reason we have been waiting and working. It's the suspense of the thing because we don't know what's inside. You're going to be fine. Let's sit down for a few minutes; we don't have to rush; nothing is going to change."

"Yes, of course, you're right," Lizzy responds, surprised at her brother's display of common sense and empathy.

65

The two sit for a few minutes and discuss the fun events of the previous evening during family time. Kevin comments on the games of checkers he enjoyed with his father. Lizzy recollects her mothers' and grandmother's comments concerning the latest social and fashion issues. And both agree they enjoy playing with little Dee at every opportunity. "Dee's disposition is so much like mothers'," Lizzy says fondly.

Soon, Lizzy feels much better and decides it's time to open the doors. She approaches the first door and turns the key, determined to see the room's contents. The door squeaks and drags slightly on the floor in protest, but Kevin reaches past Lizzy to give it a forceful push over the slightly swollen wood, and the door begins to swing open. Creeping forward in suspense with their eyes wide open, they try to navigate the darkened room.

"Do you hear soft music, Lizzy?" Kevin asks quietly.

"I hear music and whispers, too," Lizzy stutters. "I need to find the light switch; we didn't bring flashlights. What a time to forget them."

"The switch has to be in about the same place as the ones in our rooms downstairs, don't you think?" Kevin mumbles quickly.

Lizzy feels the switch and pushes the top button. Light floods the large room but stops about twenty feet in front of the children. Suddenly, there is no end to the room, no back wall within sight. Only an almost transparent veil of a mysterious, thin, vapor-like curtain with shadows of people moving on the other side and the sound of a soft waltz feigning from an unseen orchestra.

"Golly whiz," Kevin gasps. "That's the music I told you about, Lizzy. The shadows we see back there must be the victims Tucker mentioned. But he didn't tell us about all of this."

"You're right, Kevin. And we need to see what's on the other side of that barrier. It's now or never," Lizzy declares with new determination. "Come on, let's go slowly; it may not be safe for us on the other side. After all, we are flesh and blood, not spirits."

Kevin appears more frightened of the unknown than his sister and hesitates to move forward next to Lizzy. Then, he quickly catches up to her, not wanting to appear to lack courage as he did during their first confrontation with Tucker. Lizzy looks over at her brother and smiles as they walk toward the veil in the lockstep of solidarity, for better or for worse.

The voices and music seem a little louder as they reach the veil but muffled, almost as though they were coming from another room. Then, stretching her arm out as though to pierce the veil and move it aside, Lizzy discovers that it is impenetrable. The veil is impassive and steadfast.

"This is impossible," exclaims Lizzy. "The veil moves and looks like a vapor or a mist but is solid somehow."

Sensing Lizzy's frustration, Kevin, looking for some way to enter the mysterious space, calls to Lizzy. "Over here, I think I found our way in." Immediately, his sister runs to his side to see what he has discovered.

"Oh, good grief," she responds. "What is that?"

"Believe it or not, it's a door," Kevin answers. "A very narrow door, right in the middle of nowhere. And look here, this is a keyhole, and what do you want to bet that the old key will open it?"

Lizzy is astonished at the find. "Well, let me see now, a door where there is no wall, a vapor or mist-like barrier that is semi-transparent but strong enough to support a door. And the door takes the same kind of century-old key we happen to have. Pinch me, Kevin; I think I'm dreaming!"

"Try the key," Kevin urges. "I'll just bet it works."

"Well, okay, kid, here we go," Lizzy says as she inserts the key into the mysterious lock, and as she turns the key, they hear it unlock. "So this is why the keys must stay together. Alright, in we go, and keep your fingers crossed because we may need to find our way back out in a hurry!"

67

"Oh, come on, Lizzy, before I lose my nerve," Kevin demands. "My legs are turning to jelly and feel like a couple of rubber bands."

"Okay," says Lizzy. "On the count of three, we both push the door open. Not too hard now; we don't know what's on the other side. Watch your step. Now, ONE, TWO, THREE, PUSH!"

CHAPTER 18:

BEYOND THE VEIL

The narrow door swings open slowly, and as it does, the voices and music become louder and more distinguishable. A foggy mist still camouflages the shadows moving just a few yards away. Just a few more, Lizzy repeats in her mind again and again as the pair moves closer to the sounds on the other side, which they can barely hear now because their hearts are beating so loudly in their ears. The anticipation they share continues to pique as a nightmare of your worst fears would do before you can wake and shake them off. Breathing has quickened, and every instinct tells them to turn back.

Kevin reaches for Lizzy's hand, not knowing if it supports his sister or bolsters his own courage. But it doesn't matter; they have committed to unraveling a century-old mystery, and it appears that the answers to their many questions may be just beyond this curious mist.

"Lizzy," Kevin whispers, "The suspense is giving me goosebumps, and I can hardly breathe."

"It sounds like a big party of some kind," Lizzy replies in a whisper as they reach the edge of the mist. She wants to avoid drawing attention, at least until she can see more clearly.

"Yeah, well, let's hope the party isn't a monster bash of some kind," Kevin whispers. 'With our luck, it's probably our gruesome buddy Tucker and his friends. Don't forget; he's going to be mighty upset to see us with the keys before he gets the one he wants. I don't trust him, Lizzy, and I think he's very dangerous. The only reason he has cooperated so far is that he needs us. If he gets his hands on the keys, no telling what he might do."

"Stop, Kevin, one thing at a time," Lizzy counters. "We don't have time to think of Tucker right now, not when we are about to show

69

ourselves to who knows whom or what. Be ready to run back the way we came through the veil door. They can't go that far, or they would have done it long ago. So they have their limits, but then, so do we once they discover us."

Like walking through a cloud, with the feeling of a quiet breeze, they emerge on the other side of the veil, confused yet amazed. Like Alice in Wonderland, they can't believe their eyes. Surprisingly, they have stepped into a whole new era. Evidence of the early nineteenth century is all about them. They are back in time without leaving the manor.

An immense ballroom stretches out before them with an exquisitely painted ceiling depicting events as far back as the sixteenth century. The walls are lined from one end to the other with the most enormous mirrors the children have ever seen, encased in elegant gold frames. The glass ceiling to the floor reflects the thousands of colored light prisms created by the magnificent crystal chandelier hanging in the center of the room. White and gold Victorian chairs line the walls where some guests gather while waiting for the orchestra to begin the next waltz or the Allemande.

Instead of ghosts and grotesque creatures like Tucker, they are astonished to discover the beautiful people of the elite class of the early eighteen Hundreds. Every woman a thing of beauty with their long, ornate ball gowns, glistening jewelry, three-quarter length gloves, and their hair swept upon their heads, secured with gems, a diamond tiara, or another stunning ornament. Every man is a dashing sight to behold with Ruffled shirts, white gloves, tie, and tails. Each one presents a fine figure of the era. There appear to be about thirty couples dancing and milling around the outskirts of the room, acknowledging acquaintances in the manner of proper society. Ladies curtsey, and gentlemen bow. How polished and appropriate their behavior appears.

Lizzy is captivated by the gathering. "This is historical," she remarks. "We are witnessing something no one else has ever seen, and we can't tell a soul about it. It's so sad and beautiful at the same time. These are the sixty victims of the fire that nobody on earth but us will ever see. I wonder if we will remember it all when we return to our rooms.

"Holy cow, Lizzy, look at us!" Kevin says as he grabs his sister's arm. "Look at your dress, and look at this monkey suit I'm wearing; holy smokes."

Lizzy, still enchanted by the sights around them, responds with shock at the sight of her little brother in a dark brown early nineteenth-century suit… knickers, waistcoat jacket, and all. "Oh my gosh, Kevin, how did this happen?" it isn't until then that she notices the changes in her appearance. Now wearing clothes of the period, she isn't upset to find herself in a most elegant lavender dress as she observes herself in the mirrors near the corner of the room. As they stare at their reflections, The two of them look very much as though they have just stepped out of a Norman Rockwell painting.

"Well, we wanted to see what was on the other side. I guess now we know," Lizzy says nervously. "I'm just not sure what we do from here," she sighs.

Pointing to the two empty chairs along the closest wall, Kevin suggests they sit and discuss their situation quietly and try not to draw attention. "Did you notice," he says as they are finally seated, " A few of the people looked our way but didn't say anything."

"Yes, I did notice and was hoping none of them would approach us," Lizzy replies. "Do you suppose that the guests assume we belong to this household? I mean, it makes sense, though I don't think kids our age were allowed to attend a ball, even if they lived here."

Kevin accepts his sisters' explanation but then asks for more clarification. "I agree, but what about Celeste? Normally, she would have been down on the main floor or in her bedroom on the second floor."

"I think she was sneaking around," Lizzy's answer is a bit of a shock to Kevin. "No, I am not insinuating that the youngster was a little sneak, but after all, she was a normal little eight-year-old. She probably only wanted to see the ladies and gentlemen all dressed in their finest, so she defied convention and went exploring for excitement. Children

71

were forbidden to participate in so many things back then, so she sneaked up the stairs but unfortunately saw Tucker do his dastardly deed, which is what led to her death."

Suddenly, Lizzy stands up and begins to pace back and forth quickly in front of Kevin as though remembering something very crucial and exciting. "Oh my goodness, Kevin, I don't know why it didn't dawn on me before this. I'm so glad you asked about Celeste. She is one of the victims, so she must be here somewhere. We need to investigate and see where some of these doors lead to; maybe we can find her. Just think, if we can, she may talk to us. Do you agree?" Lizzy asks, enthused at the possibility of connecting their two worlds through the youngest victim.

"Capital idea Lizzy," Kevin exclaims. "A really great idea! We could learn so much from her before finding out exactly how to release all of the victims. None of them seem too upset with their arrangement right now, but after this long, no doubt they have given up and been making the best of a bad situation."

"I'm sure you're right," professes Lizzy. One hundred and forty-something years will change a person's perceptions and values. We need to see if we can navigate the labyrinth behind these other doors. More passionate and determined than ever to succeed, the two-time travelers develop a feasible plan for their search, including a way to track their route, making retreat easier when needed.

Kevin looks at his watch to see if there is enough time left to choose a door and begin their search for Celeste. "We can't go any further now," he says, pointing to the time. "We will have to go back the way we came. We don't dare be late for dinner, or there will be questions we can't answer from Grandmother Hannah and father. It's going to take time to get through the veil, lock the narrow door, the room door, get cleaned up, and be downstairs before they announce dinner."

Lizzy knows that her brother is right, though every fiber of her being wants to stay and begin looking for the little girl who knows what happened that fateful night. But they will have to postpone that opportunity until tomorrow.

"Okay, Kevin, let's start on our way back now. We can come back in the morning, though I doubt that either one of us will be able to sleep much tonight.

The children begin their trek back into the present. They found the narrow door and made sure it was securely locked behind them using the original key.

"Look, Lizzy, our clothes have changed back again," Kevin noticed as they reached the door to the gallery.

Locking it up again, they turn around to see Tucker blown up to what looks like twice his original size and twice as hideous and angry as ever. Indescribable colors swirl around the wretched form, and his eyes glow bright blood red to match his rage. His voice thunders loud enough to rattle the banister rail on the stairway.

"Give me those keys!" he bellows. "You had them all the time, and now I want them. You won't get away from me this time unless you hand them over to me."

"No!" screams Lizzy. "I will use the key to send you back to where you belong, but you cannot have the keys. The keys have to stay together, don't you understand? If they are separated, one will not work without the other, and I will not let you have both keys. There's too much at stake, and I don't trust you. You don't care if the other victims make it back to their origins or not, but we are going to see to it that they are released, and that includes you."

Meanwhile, unnoticed by Tucker, Kevin has slipped past him and is standing near the top of the stairway—Kevin motions for Lizzy to throw him the keys.

"I said give me those keys, or you will be a very sorry little girl," Tucker roars as he stands over Lizzy.

Lizzy quickly moves to one side and tosses the keys to Kevin. Tucker's attention follows the airborne keys while Lizzy runs past him toward the stairs. "You can't have them," she yells. "And you might be big, but you're slow," she adds—Kevin motions for her to continue running toward the stairway. Then, the two disappear to the floor below as Tucker paces back and forth at the top of the stairs.

CHAPTER 19:

PART-TIME SLEUTHS

Arriving at the dinner table, still breathless from their encounter with Tucker and the rush to be on time, the novice detectives are thankful for family and scrumptious meals.

Afterward, the rest of the family adjourns to the living room for shared relaxation and time to discuss the day's events. Lizzy and Kevin separate from the adults for a few minutes and go to the small library.

"What a day!" Kevin proclaims. "I never in my life would have dreamed of such a day. I still couldn't explain it to anyone, even if I had the chance. They would think I was out of my mind, and I couldn't blame them. A heavy mist INSIDE the house? Really? Under the same roof, two time periods more than a century apart? A ghastly ghost with the personality of Jack the Ripper? I don't think so! And last but not least, let's not forget the huge, elaborate ballroom filled with sixty lovely people who happen to be dead! Oh, and I almost forgot the instant wardrobe change. Nope, nobody would believe a word of it, and right this minute, I'm not so sure I believe it either, and I was there!"

Meanwhile, Lizzy sits with her hand over her mouth to keep from laughing out loud at her brother's blunt descriptions of the day's discoveries. She knows it all sounds too ridiculous to be accurate, and no one would believe a word. It's just as well because all she wants is to send Tucker and the other victims back where they belong so they and the residents of Stuart Manor can have peace. But first, there is much more to do. She surmises that she and Kevin will often be in and out of that gorgeous ballroom.

"Kevin, we need to move to the living room before the others are irritated because we didn't follow," warns Lizzy. "We don't want them to shut us down. We have come too far, and I'm excited about what we may find while looking for Celeste."

Joining the adults, the two cannot truthfully share their day with everyone, so Lizzy keeps busy reading books to Dee. Jessica and Hannah enjoy a game of checkers while Kevin and Marshal continue the chess game that they began two nights ago. About an hour later, Dee is sleepy and needs to be carried upstairs to bed, so everyone decides to call it a night.

Kevin waits until the adults have gone to their rooms and then taps on Lizzy's door. "What is it?" asks Lizzy as she peeks around the partially open door.

"I just wanted to warn you not to be too surprised if we hear a lot of noise in the middle of the night," Kevin remarks. "Old Tucker was pretty mad at us, so it would be just like him to create a disturbance to annoy us. If he does, don't even think about coming to get me to go with you upstairs because it's not going to happen. I need sleep, and so do you, and he can't come down here, so plug your ears and go back to sleep if he starts something. We can deal with him in the morning."

"Okay," replies Lizzy. "I didn't think I would be this tired tonight, but I feel like I could sleep for a week. I'll see you in the morning. Sleep tight, don't let the bed bugs bite," Lizzy teases, closes the door and curls up in bed. Kevin, pleased with getting Lizzy to agree to his terms, returns to his room to do the same.

Asleep almost before her head touches the pillow, Lizzy's last thoughts are retaliation against Tucker if he causes a commotion during the night. She vows to personally punch him in the nose in the morning, provided he has a nose. She doesn't remember seeing one.

The following morning, while waking up from an uneventful night's sleep, Lizzy enjoys one of her favorite things about mornings at Stuart Manor. The soft, clean breeze coming through her bedroom window carries with it the bright, cheery songs of the birds that frequent the grounds. How happy and carefree they sound as they gather at the feeders hanging in the trees close to the house.

Fighting the urge to lay in bed all day, Lizzy forces herself to prepare for breakfast and the day ahead. She remembers that today could be critical if she and Kevin find Celeste.

And then there's Tucker, she thinks to herself. What a bully! But something bothers her about him, and she can't put her finger on it. Something just doesn't fit. He's a big, annoying fellow, alright, but so far, it's been a lot of blustering and noise, which doesn't make sense. His intimidation felt more threatening before she and Kevin found the keys. Now, he seems more vicious, but it's all for effect. Why is that? She questions this over and over. If I were a monster like Tucker, she thinks, and I knew someone had the key on them that they refuse to give up, why wouldn't I push them down and take the key away from them? Why wait for anyone to hand it to me if I wanted it that bad? "Strange," she says aloud. "I think Kevin and I need to figure this out if we can. And one more thing, why does nobody in the house seem to hear all the noise Tucker makes? Neither the family nor staff have mentioned hearing anything out of the ordinary."

At breakfast, Marshal gets the undivided attention of his two mini detectives by mentioning the school subject.

"School, father? But school doesn't begin until fall, which is months away," Lizzy reacts. The very last thing on the children's minds lately is school.

"You must prepare to take entrance exams before school begins," Marshal explains. "Because we took you out of your last school so abruptly, you were unable to complete your courses with the mandatory examinations for your records. Your grades were satisfactory, but testing is required before registering for the new year into the grade level for which you qualify. The supervised exams are scheduled for next month, and your mother has the list of subjects. Therefore, you will dedicate your mornings, starting tomorrow, to the study of these subjects, so you are prepared. Any questions?"

"Golly, it just seems like such short notice," Kevin declares; though it is unlikely he will have any trouble prepping for the tests, schoolwork comes easy. On the other hand, Lizzy will have to study harder and not let her mind wander into another daydream. She's an intelligent young lady but loses control of her imagination from time to time.

"Don't get anxious about it," warns Marshal. "If you study hard in the mornings, the time will pass quickly; before you know it, the exams will be over, and you can go on with your summer activities."

"Little does he know," Lizzy whispers to Kevin. "Studying is not the problem. The problem is rushing in the afternoons to find Celeste and solve some of our mysteries. I think we should start going to bed earlier to begin studying earlier in the morning. That will leave us a little more time to look around the third floor in the afternoons.

"I guess we don't have a choice," agrees Kevin. "We do have to pass those tests so we can work it all out some way. It's only for a month. So starting tomorrow, we are part-time detectives," he says with a mischievous grin.

"Well, we do have the whole day today," Lizzy reminds Kevin. "Maybe we'll find Celeste behind one of those doors in the ballroom. I sure hope so because I think she can answer our questions about the fire and the state of limbo or oblivion that she and the others have existed in all this time. I feel certain she will know how we can release all the poor souls to have peace. And I'm also certain she knows how we can handle Tucker when he's in one of those outrageous fits he likes to exhibit. It will help a lot if we know how to neutralize him."

"Good thinking, Lizzy. Let's get our things together and get started," Kevin says with a tone of urgency. "We don't want to waste the only full day we have. I think it's going to be a fascinating day!"

CHAPTER 20:

FINDING CELESTE

Resolved to accomplish as much as possible during this last full day of exploring, Lizzy and Kevin gather the keys and a few other supplies before starting up the stairs to the third floor.

"I wonder if Tucker is lurking around already this morning," Lizzy mumbles. "Isn't it odd that he never seems to be active early in the morning? I'll tell you, Kevin, there are a few things I can't figure out about him. He gets so angry and threatens violence but never carries through, thank goodness, and we know he can go through the walls from room to room where the others are but cannot walk through the locked doors to the gallery.

"Yeah, he's strange, alright," Kevin adds. By the way, before I forget about it, did you notice that there were no clocks when we were on the other side of the veil? It made me wonder if time passes at all in that world but only on this side of the veil."

"Whoa, creepy!" Lizzy gasps, but it could explain a lot; I don't know what yet. Okay, here's the door we go through. Let's not waste any more time."

Lizzy opens the door with the newer key, and the pair find themselves back in the dimly lit room containing the mysterious veil at the far end, exactly where it was the first time. Carefully, they walk forward, hoping there will be no surprises as they begin their probing again.

The misty veil is as astonishing to experience as the first time. Never really sure of themselves, the twosome soak up the strange environment as the pair pass through the narrow door, locking it behind them once again. The scenario hasn't changed since yesterday. Couples are dancing and visiting all over the magnificent ballroom, and the children's attire is also the same amazing costumes of the era. Lizzy is pleased to wear the pretty lavender dress, while Kevin expresses his displeasure about wearing the brown suit with knickers once again. "No wonder there are no clocks here; everything stays the same," he mutters.

Lizzy chimes in, "You're right; a person would hardly know if and when they missed a day. Let's get started. We can walk down the left side of the room where two of the three doors are. We can try the nearest door first. We have to start somewhere, and I have a hunch we're on the right track."

"I'm right behind you, girl," Kevin agrees.

Trying to look aloof, as though they belonged among the grandeur and distinction of the period, the children move to the nearest of the three doors. Lizzy quietly turns the handle and begins to enter the next room, while Kevin, with his back to his sister, keeps a watchful eye to see if they are being followed. After closing the door, he uses his pocket knife to carve a small niche in an inconspicuous place on the door frame to mark it if they must backtrack later.

"Oh my goodness," Kevin hears his sister say as he turns around to join her.

They are standing on a white veranda with massive pillars and furnished with every type of casual furniture comfort. A few people are seated, but many stand at the front railing to watch the activities. Stretched out in front of the veranda are lawns and gardens for hundreds of yards. Several croquet games are in progress throughout the grounds and also archery lessons. Everyone seems to be enjoying themselves in the sunshine. A few remain seated in the shade, relaxed and reading. The door they chose is an exit, but there is something artificial about the scene.

"L-i-z-z-y," Kevin drags the name out slowly as though cautioning her not to move too fast or speak too loudly.

Lizzy freezes in place, afraid to move. "What's the matter?" she asks softly.

"Take a good look at the people out here," he answers. Look at them carefully and see if you notice anything peculiar.

Lizzy scans the area slowly, looking at the small crowd intently to see what it is that Kevin finds so strange. They seem like very nice people to her, and she wonders where the additional children are from.

"What is it, Kevin? I don't see anything wrong." She says, irritated because they need to be looking for Celeste.

"Okay," Kevin replies. "Now go back to the door we just came through and take a good look at the people and see if there is anyone you recognize."

"Oh, Kevin, we don't have time for this," Lizzy snaps.

"Just do it," he insists.

Exasperated with the situation, Lizzy walks the few steps to the door and looks in. She examines the faces, beautiful gowns, and handsome escorts. One gentleman reminds her of her uncle Howard, which brings back memories. But still unsure of what it is that alarms Kevin, she returns to him on the veranda.

"Kevin, I don't understand what you want me to see, and we need to be looking for Celeste," she delivers in an annoyed and frustrated tone.

"Okay, just hold on, Lizzy, and come walk with me," Kevin keeps his voice patronizing as he ushers his sister out onto the lawns and among the guests. In a few minutes, the expression on Lizzy's face changes from irritation to shock as she turns and looks for a chair.

"I can't believe my eyes," she exclaims a little louder than intended. "These are the same people as the ones in the ballroom! How can that be?" Does that mean we will find the same people behind the other two doors in the ballroom?

"Very possibly," Kevin answers. I read about something like this somewhere. It didn't make sense then, but I think I understand better now. Everything we're seeing is actually in a different dimension. "Have you noticed that we are outdoors, but there is no air? What we

81

are breathing is the same as the air indoors at the house. There are no breezes here. Everything is still, like in a painting, except for the people milling around. No animals, no birds. It's uncanny!"

"Let's Walk around here some more; maybe someone can tell us where to find Celeste."

Lizzy and her brother walk the outskirts of the guests, hoping to spot someone who looks like they are of the old staff or maybe a nanny. They watch a few children play, hoping to spot the little eight-year-old girl with the answers they need.

Sighting a couple of footmen standing under a large tent, prepared to serve lemonade and hors d'oeuvre, the couple decides to ask them for information.

"Can you tell us where we might find Miss Celeste?" Lizzy asks as if she is a friend of the family.

"I'm sorry, Miss Lizzy, but Miss Celeste wouldn't be among these guests. However, you might try the playroom inside," answers one of the footmen.

Lizzy thanks the footman and begins to leave. Suddenly, she turns sharply around and confronts him.

"How did you know my name? How do you know who we are?" She demands.

"You don't recognize me, Miss Lizzy?" the footman teases in a menacing tone. "You know who I am, and we will meet again as usual." Then he leaves to tend to a guest.

"Oh, good heavens, that was Tucker!" Kevin proclaims. "So that's what he's supposed to look like."

Struggling for words through a fog of disbelief, Lizzy finally finds the word to describe this ghoulish adventure. "Bizarre!"

"Come on, Lizzy, let's find the playroom," Kevin says, wanting to get both of them out of this freakish situation and back on the trail. And she agrees that just about any place is better than here right now.

The playroom must be behind one of the other doors; the pair walk back to the veranda and through the door to the ballroom again. Two doors are left to select. One more door remains on the left side of the ballroom, and the third door is directly across on the right side. Lizzy decides to cross the floor to the right side, hoping Celeste and the playroom are inside.

"Well, Kevin, keep your fingers crossed. I don't think either one of us wants any of this to go on much longer.

"And a hearty Amen to that," Kevin responds. "It's getting too gruesome for me."

The door opens into a hallway, and all seems peaceful enough. There are four rooms before the hall empties into a large living area of some kind at the other end.

"Shh, Kevin, listen," Lizzy says as she strains to hear. Soon it becomes more apparent; the sound of a little girl humming seems to be from the next room down the hallway. Lizzy and her brother hold their breath and hope as they approach the open doorway. They stop outside the room so they don't startle the girl they see inside. She looks to be about Kevin's age, but she is sitting with her back to the door and engrossed in painting a picture of the bouquet of wildflowers she has sitting on a pedestal just beyond and to the right side of her easel.

"Hello," says Lizzy softly. I hope we aren't disturbing you.

"Oh, hello," the girl says as she stands up. Can I help you with something?" she asks pleasantly.

"Well, we are looking for a young lady by the name of Celeste. Do you happen to be her?" Lizzy asks hopefully.

"Yes, I am Celeste," the girl answers, much to the relief of the two searchers. "Wait, are you from the main house, the Stuart manor?" she continues.

"Yes, we are," Lizzy and her brother answer together. "We are so happy to find you finally. You see, we found a note your sister Angela left in the pocket of a smock. We had to solve a riddle to find the keys that would lead us to you. I'm sure we can help you and the others, and you could help us by answering some of our questions about things only you would know. That is if you're willing."

"I will be glad to help you, but can it wait until tomorrow afternoon? We can meet back here."

"Oh, that would be wonderful, Celeste! We appreciate it so much. By the way, my name is Lizzy Stuart, and this is my brother Kevin. Well, we will let you get back to your lovely painting and will go back to the house. We'll see you tomorrow afternoon, then."

"It has been so nice meeting you both," Celeste says as the pair leave the room to go back to the ballroom and trace their steps back to the veil and the gallery.

"What a nice girl she seems to be. I can hardly wait until tomorrow," Kevin says excitedly.

CHAPTER 21:

THE LOCKET

With the materials they need for home study, Lizzie and Kevin begin their work immediately following an early breakfast. Jessica supplies her children with the subjects required to pass the exams next month and the grade averages needed to avoid repeating a year.

Both children are determined to do well to please their parents, if for no other reason. But they do have a secondary motive, of course, which is the task of rescuing the sixty souls on the third floor, including the one guilty of creating this impossible situation in the first place.

Lizzy and Kevin are comfortable dedicating their time between breakfast and lunch to their studies. It won't be too difficult because their teachers in Texas have already covered most of the topics, and there are short studies for the few they have missed.

On this first morning of their new routine, the would-be investigators have agreed to study with no interruptions and no clowning or audible remarks that would distract each other.

Four hours and some head-scratching later, Mrs. Kelly taps on the study room door and announces lunch. Not having to be told twice, the students are more than ready to abandon the books for today. They head for the dining room, where Jessica turns them around and insists they wash their hands and face before eating.

Lunch is delicious as usual, and to celebrate the children's dedication to their studies, Mrs. Kelly offers her rich chocolate nut brownies with a scoop of vanilla ice cream as a reward. There are no fools in this family; they dig into the treat without a word.

"Oh me, I think I might burst," Kevin moans while pushing himself away from the table while the others laugh and tease.

"I'm raising piggies," Jessica teases. "Okay, you two go into the living room and sit for a while to let that big lunch settle. We don't want any stomach aches today, do we?"

Thirty minutes later, Lizzy and her brother gather their things to take to the third floor. Both are anxious to end this adventure, which has proved to have some eerie twists. But they made promises they must keep.

Once again, the children climb the stairs, let themselves into the dim room, and unlock the narrow door. Passing through the veil to the other side and locking the door behind them, they continue toward the door to take them to the hallway and Celeste's playroom.

Out of nowhere, Tucker, the footman, grabs Lizzy's arm and twists it enough to force her to drop the keys. Quickly, he bends and reaches for them, but Kevin is faster and now angry because of what this creep has done to his sister.

"Take your hands off of her, or I swear I will destroy these keys. I will take them to the main house and destroy them, and you will remain here for eternity," demands Kevin. Tucker can see that the boy means every word, so he lets go of Lizzy's arm.

"Oh, I was just kidding, boy. I didn't mean any harm. Can't you see that I was just having fun with you? I wouldn't hurt your sister," Tucker pleads.

"I don't believe a word you say," Kevin retorts. "Now you go on your way, and don't bother us again, or I promise you, you will rot here forever."

"I'm going; I'm going. But I'll get even, don't think I won't. I'll get even," Tucker bellows and leaves just as abruptly as he came.

Both children are shaken and worried about what Tucker meant about getting even, but now they must keep their appointment with Celeste so they can end this nightmare.

Celeste is waiting in the playroom when they arrive. They apologize for being a little late and tell her of the incident with Tucker. She nods her head and smiles; she knows full well what Tucker is capable of doing.

"I'm sorry that our situation here has put you both in so much trouble and danger," Celeste continues. "But you see, there has been no way for any of us in this dimension to know or help. Tucker is the only one who can go on to the gallery. All of us can go from room to room as long as what we touch or use is from the past, but we cannot go through a doorway that leads to the gallery. That area is in a different dimension. Tucker can access it for some reason, but the rest of us cannot. However, he cannot enter the storeroom or the gallery as a butler, but only as the tormented remains you have often seen because that is where he came back to and perished as a criminal. On the other hand, I was able to lay out my father's uniform and the pinafore. I knew about the note that Angela put in the pocket, bless her heart."

"Wow, who would believe it," Kevin blurts out. "No offense, but we promised to release all of you so you can go where you will have peace. Please help us to do that as quickly as possible."

"Bless you both," Celeste responds with tears in her eyes. "Lizzy, this is for you to open now," she says as she hands Lizzy a tiny white box with a cameo picture on top of the lid.

"Oh my, you don't have to give us anything," The gift humbles Lizzy. She opens the little box to find a small locket and chain inside. The locket has the same cameo picture on the front of it. "This is beautiful," she says and places it around her neck, asking Kevin to fasten it for her.

"Now," Celeste continues. "You must not take it off for any reason until your mission is complete. You must have it with you at all times. As long as you wear that locket and carry the two keys together, not Tucker or anyone else can take the keys from you. You see, the narrow door is our way out of this dimension and our passage home. But we cannot touch the key to unlock that door. The plan only works one way for both dimensions. We must all be ready to leave with you leading the way. You will unlock the narrow door and pass through, but don't lock it on the other side; it must be left open, and we will wait at the opening. Then, you will unlock the gallery door and pass through. Now, this is very, very important! Listen carefully! You will have only five minutes to reach the gallery door, pass through, and close the door. When you close the gallery door and lock it with the new key, the dimensions will meld into one, allowing each of us to walk through the narrow door and back to where we belong. Do not unlock the gallery door again until the old key disappears and you are left with only the new key in your hand. When that happens, all of us will be safely out of the manor permanently."

"Oh my gosh," Lizzy says breathlessly. "That is so amazing. It is so serious, it sounds difficult, but it isn't, is it?" She is trembling at the thought of the responsibility while Kevin has been listening in jaw-dropping disbelief and says nothing.

Celeste asks about the arrangements. "When do you want to do this? Everyone will be so excited when I announce your plans."

Lizzy's head is spinning, and she knows she must have at least one day to clear her thinking before they complete the mission.

"Celeste, can your people be ready to go the day after tomorrow in the afternoon at about two O'clock?" If so, I think it will work out fine then.

"Well, Lizzy," Celeste says with a grin, time stands still for us, so when you come, we will all be there, even Tucker."

"Oh, I see," says Lizzy, forgetting there are no clocks in this dimension. "Okay, then it's settled. We will be back the day after tomorrow at two O'clock our time, and then you will all be free to go home at last.

"That sounds like heaven," Celeste answers, holding back the flood of tears she knows are coming. "Goodbye for now, and God bless you."

Lizzy and Kevin leave the room and backtrack to their exit path, not stopping until they are in the gallery again with the doors locked behind them. Worn out mentally from listening to Celeste's explanations, they both need to sit down for a while and try to make heads or tails out of everything they heard. Kevin suggests they go to the small library, where the sofas and chairs are overstuffed and comfortable.

CHAPTER 22:

THE EXODUS

"Wow, imagine being stuck like that, confined to those rooms with no real hope to hang on to," Keven sighs. "I suppose it is merciful to be without time in their case. Otherwise, it would surely drive a person mad. I know I couldn't take it."

"Well, the plan isn't really very complicated and should go off without a problem," he continues. "That is unless Tucker thinks of some way to mess everything up. Boy, I was mad at him for grabbing you like that. He's so big; I'm not sure what I could have done to stop him. I'm just glad he believed I would destroy the keys."

I really appreciate what you did, Kevin," Lizzy says with sincerity while wiping a tear from her eye. "That was the first time he had ever touched one of us, so now we don't know what to expect. But when I think about it, Celeste will probably tell him along with the others, tomorrow, if she hasn't already. Tucker should be happy with the news like everyone else, so he may not make any trouble at all."

"Let's hope not," says Kevin, smiling and crossing his fingers for luck. "You know what, Lizzy? In a couple of days, we will be able to open all the doors on the third floor from one end of the hallway to the other all at once if we want to—no telling what we could find inside those rooms. And we can tell Grandmother Hannah where we found the new key, and she will be able to sort through everything for the tourists and the museum.

Lizzy and Kevin go to their rooms almost immediately after dinner to relax and forget the day's ordeal. Lizzy wants to return to the novel she began reading a week ago, and Kevin will tackle the new airplane model his father bought him yesterday. They will have nothing but their school studies to concentrate on tomorrow.

90

Following breakfast the next morning, Jessica goes to the study room with the children to test them briefly on the subjects they have been revisiting. Fortunately, the Stuart -Children are like sponges and have soaked up and retained the work they have completed so far. Satisfied with their progress, Jessica leaves them to their studies and stops to tell her husband how well they are progressing.

The afternoon is perfect for enjoying the outdoors, so Lizzy and Kevin take Dee for a walk and playtime just between the three of them. One afternoon totally different than any Lizzy and Kevin have enjoyed lately. Still, they look forward to tomorrow afternoon and the completion of their promise to release the victims who have been captive for so long. Tomorrow they will all be where they belong and rest in peace. Tonight, the young investigators will sleep well, and tomorrow they will do what they know is right.

Awakened by the aroma of bacon, pancakes, and hot maple syrup, Lizzy dresses quickly and runs down the hall to wake her brother. "Get up, sleepyhead, and follow your nose," she says, tapping loudly on his door and giggling. "Mrs. Kelly has done it again!"

Four hours of study and lunchtime go by quickly when their concentration is frequently interrupted by thoughts of the upcoming task and how important a successful outcome will be to so many. Lizzy and Kevin just want to do their best and get it completed.

"It's one forty-five," Kevin alerts Lizzy. "Fifteen minutes to get upstairs and to the door in the veil."

"I'm ready," Lizzy answers, enthused but nervous. "Let's go."

Opening the third-floor room door, everything in the dimly lit room looks the same. "I guess this is the last time we will see this room quite the same," Kevin supposes. As usual, stretched out before them is the same large room with the misty veil at the other end. The children walk a little faster this time, knowing what will happen when they reach the narrow door. Without a word, and their hearts beating faster than ever before, they reach the door, and Lizzy nervously fumbles with the key. They can hear voices on the other side, so they know that everyone is ready to go. Finally, the door swings open to a crowd of faces, wet with tears and arms outstretched, offering hugs to their rescuers. Celeste stands in front to greet Lizzy and Kevin. Behind her stands Tucker, the footman with head bowed. The crowd nervously awaits the moment they can cross through the narrow door into a peaceful eternity. Neither Celeste, Lizzy, or Kevin can speak. Emotions are high, but now is the time for action. Lizzy blows a kiss to the crowd, and the children walk quickly back to the gallery door. They exit onto the gallery quickly, turn, and lock the door with the new key. Then Lizzy and Kevin stare at Lizzy's hand to watch for the old key to disappear as Celeste said it would when all the victims were safely through the portal and on their way home. Two minutes, three minutes, five minutes, the key appears to be fading. Then, for six minutes, only an outline of the key remains for a few seconds and then disappears completely.

"They're gone," Lizzy says almost sadly. "They're gone, Tucker's gone, and the nightmare is finally over. My goodness, I feel lighter, like a ton of weight has been lifted off my shoulders."

"It's a big relief, alright," says Kevin, still humbled by the memory of the crowd who were so grateful. "Should we open the door and look in?" he asks.

"No, not today," Lizzy replies quickly. "Let's leave it for later. There's no rush now. We can tell Grandmother Hannah that we found the new key and that tomorrow, we will unlock all the doors on the third floor. Besides, for some reason, I am so tired. I would really like a nice long nap about now. I think I'll go to my room and lay down awhile."

"Lizzy! Lizzy darling! Lizzy, wake up, sweetheart. Talk to me, sweetie, it's mother. Open your eyes and talk to your mother! Oh, Marshal, I'm frightened!" Lizzy hears her mother's frantic voice and wonders what's wrong but cannot seem to concentrate.

"Don't be frightened, Mrs. Stuart; your little girl is going to be just fine. She's not seriously hurt, just banged up a little, and her wounds should heal nicely. Of course, that knot on her head will stay swollen for a couple of days, and concussions can be serious, but I don't think there is any lasting damage. She will have headaches for a few days and be mighty sore for a while. I want to see her in my office for a few x-rays soon."

"Thank you, doctor Spence," Jessica says between sobs. "Look, I think she is waking up! Lizzy, Lizzy darling, look at Mother, let me see your beautiful big eyes."

Lizzy struggles to open her eyes which seem like tiny narrow slits that she can barely see through. And her eyelids are so heavy. Her head hurts, and everything else that she tries to move. "Mother," she mumbles through swollen lips. "Mother, where are you? What's happened? Did I fall down the stairs? Where's Kevin?

"Mother's right here, sweetheart," Jessica answers. "And here's father too, can you see him, dear? Don't worry; you're going to be just fine. Kevin is here too."

"Kevin," Lizzy mumbles. "Kevin, do you have the key? Did I fall and drop the new key?"

"What key?" Kevin answers.

"You know, the new key we had left after the old one finally disappeared," Lizzy struggles to explain.

"I'm sorry, Lizzy, but I don't know what you're talking about," Kevin replies but thinks Lizzy must have been dreaming, or the injury has her mixed up.

"Miss Lizzy, my name is Doctor Spence. Now, I want you to lay still and rest as much as you can. Your father has sent someone to the drugstore to fill a prescription. The pills will help you feel better and also help you sleep. I don't want you to worry because you are a tough little girl, and you're going to be just fine."

"What happened Mother" Lizzy asks. "How did I get hurt?"

"Well, sweetie," Jessica begins. "When we drove up to the house, you were halfway out of the open window of the limousine trying to see how high it is to the top of the manor. When the limousine stopped under the portal, you fell out of the window. You landed on the luggage carrier one of the servants brought out and then hit your head on the base of a concrete column. You have been unconscious for almost an hour now. You scared us to death. It was a nasty fall, and you do have a mild concussion. Doctor Spence says you will be sore for quite a while, but you're going to be fine. Nothing broken, just banged up a lot."

"I don't remember being in the limousine except for the day Grandmother Hannah picked us up from the railway station," Lizzy stammers.

"Yes, dear, that was this morning," Jessica explains, but she can see the apparent confusion on her daughter's face.

"This morning?" Lizzy questions. "No, mother, that can't be. We have been living here for almost two months now. Kevin and I have been studying for the exams we have to take next month for school in the fall. He and I have been exploring the third floor of this house where the fire took place in 1807, and sorted out all of the trunks and suitcases left in the storeroom for grandmother to use for display when the tourists come. And we found the key to the new doors that replaced the ones burned during the fire. We found the keys behind a portrait at the top of the stairs at the third-floor landing."

"Lizzy, listen to me," Jessica is certain now that her daughter has been having dreams or nightmares while unconscious. "Listen, darling; It's all been a dream. The fall knocked you out, and you have been semi-conscious and delirious since then. Everything you just told us is part of a dream. Honest sweetie, we wouldn't lie to you, and you know how real dreams can sometimes be. You must understand that, sweetheart. It was all a dream! You're waking up from a long, bad dream. Now, I want you to rest, and when you're ready, I'll help you get some soup in your stomach. We will have to use a straw because a spoon isn't going to work with that fat lip you have right now," Jessica says with a smile.

"I'll rest in a minute, mother, but right now, I want to talk to Kevin privately. It's alright, really. I just need to straighten out some things in my head, and he can help," Lizzy coaxes. Her mother and the others leave Kevin and Lizzy alone.

"It all seems so real," Lizzy tells Kevin. I seem to remember everything so clearly. Just answer a few questions for me, would you please?"

"Sure, Lizzy," Kevin responds, concerned about his sister's injuries but wanting her to understand everything so she can rest.

"Tell me, "She begins, "What about all the time you and I spent looking for the two keys for the third-floor bedroom doors? And what about Tucker? Is Tucker part of my imagination, too?

Kevin listens closely to the questions but cannot make himself understand the connections between Lizzy's questions and her accident.

"Lizzy, you know I have never lied to you. Well, I don't know anything about keys or bedrooms on the third floor, and who is this Tucker person?" Kevin answers as honestly as he knows how. "None of those things happened and are all just a bad dream you had between your fall and when you woke a few minutes ago. But I'll say, it sounds like an exciting dream."

Following a few more questions, to try and sort reality from her imagination, Lizzy is saddened to realize that all her memories of a really great mystery investigation only took place inside her head.

"Too bad you weren't there," Lizzy tells Kevin with a swollen grin. "It was a really awesome adventure!"

Imagination is a creative gift from God!

ABOUT THE AUTHOR

Sandra S. Rose

Sandra S."Rusty" Rose was born in the South, and currently resides in Florida's "Sunshine State". Following high school graduation, she enlisted in the Women's Army Corps where she acquired valuable training in business, finance, and self-discipline. Her assignments taught her the value of extensive, thorough research. Deciding against a 20-year military career, she returned home to advance her education and enter a successful 30-year career as an Executive Writer and Professional Grant Writer.

Now retired, she has the opportunity to pursue her love of writing for enjoyment. With a deep love for God, Family, and Country, Sandra seeks to use her vivid imagination to produce material that readers of all ages will enjoy. She aspires to offer up additional publications in the future, both in Fiction and Nonfiction efforts.

BOOKS BY THIS AUTHOR

Funding Your Nonprofit

A Guide to successful grant writing. Millions of dollars are available to nonprofits, entrepreneurs and other businesses 24/7. Money made possible through the government, private and public Foundations and other philanthropic resources across the world.

Shadows On The Third Floor

Shadows: In the Spring of 1954, Marshal Stuart abruptly uproots his family of five from Houston, Texas, to relocate to Boston, Massachusetts. The rationale is unclear to his three children, which heightens the mystery

Lizzy, the family's twelve-year-old adventuress, and her nine-year-old brother Kevin are junior sleuths and soon find the mysteries of their new residence a real and dangerous challenge to their investigative skills.

Late-night confrontations with hideous, surreal beings threaten the children's progress of solving the mystery of a century old tragedy.

Madeleine; *What Doesn't Kill You Makes You Stronger*

An infant, unwanted by her parents is raised 12 years by loving grandparents. The child is cherished and taught that respect for others builds self-respect also. Her happy, kind and gentle nature makes others around her happy until she is ripped away from those she loves. Battered and abused for years, she later enlists in the military.

Afterward, life presents a series of trials she must overcome, making her stronger in areas where most women fear to tread. Madeleine must tackle traumatic situations in adulthood when evil raises its head in her own home. Tenacity becomes her middle name as she meets every challenge with more strength and determination than the last.

Made in the USA
Monee, IL
02 December 2024

71820942R00059